the LOVE EMERGENCY series

EMERGENCY
Attraction

the **LOVE EMERGENCY** series

EMERGENCY
Attraction

USA TODAY BESTSELLING AUTHOR
SAMANTHE BECK

This book is a work of fiction. Names, characters, places, and incidents are the product of the author's imagination or are used fictitiously. Any resemblance to actual events, locales, or persons, living or dead, is coincidental.

Copyright © 2017 by Samanthe Beck. All rights reserved, including the right to reproduce, distribute, or transmit in any form or by any means. For information regarding subsidiary rights, please contact the Publisher.

Entangled Publishing
644 Shrewsbury Commons Ave
STE 181
Shrewsbury, PA 17361
rights@entangledpublishing.com

Brazen is an imprint of Entangled Publishing.

Edited by Heather Howland
Cover design by LJ Anderson/Mayhem Cover Creations
Cover photography from IgorVetushko/Deposit Photos

Manufactured in the United States of America

First Edition April 2017

ENTANGLED
BRAZEN

To anyone who has ever needed a second chance.

Chapter One

"Son of a bitch…"

Sinclair Smith swallowed the rest of the expletives lodged in her throat and watched her worst mistake cross the room. He caught her looking. The lying lips once responsible for making her heart race and her clothes fall off kicked up at one corner. It didn't matter that she hadn't laid eyes on Shane Maguire in ten years. She'd know that slow, unrepentant smile anywhere, even in the bustle of her sister Savannah's wedding reception.

"Problem?"

The question came from the man sitting beside her—best man Hunter Knox—and reminded her the rest of the room hadn't actually disappeared. John Legend's "All of Me" transitioned to The Beatles' "In My Life," and the DJ invited everyone to join the happy couple on the dance floor. Shane continued his unhurried strides, as if she'd been sitting there for the past decade, patiently waiting for him to show up and turn her world upside down. Again.

"No problem," she replied. Without taking her eyes off

Shane, she grabbed Hunter's hand. "Dance with me." The tall, strapping EMT had inches and pounds on her, but surprise worked in her favor. She hauled him to the center of the dance floor, slung her arms over his broad shoulders and fit herself against him like she belonged there. When she looked beyond him, she had the satisfaction of seeing Shane stop in his tracks. His eyes narrowed, and then…whoa. Her view spun away as Hunter executed a fluid move and reversed their position.

Rather than crane her neck, and give Shane the mistaken impression she gave an actual crap what he did, she switched her attention to her partner. Hunter was a hottie, with his clear blue eyes and easy grin. Given the opportunity, she might have been interested in finding out exactly how good the best man really was, but Savannah had told her he was crazy in love with some lucky girl. Thankfully, she wasn't looking for crazy, or love. She just needed a compliant dance partner—which he wasn't turning out to be. He resisted every attempt she made to take the lead. "Hey, Footloose, what are you doing?"

"Trying to size up the guy you're aiming to make jealous." His voice held no complaint, just curiosity.

She almost laughed out loud. "I'm not aiming to make anyone jealous. I wouldn't waste my time on such a stupid game."

Dark blond brows lifted. "You don't play games?"

"Oh, I *can* play games." Giving in, she craned her neck and scanned the crowd. "I can play with the best of them. I'm simply not playing one now. I'm not interested in speaking with someone—someone who's not supposed to be here in the first place—much less dancing with him. I figure the best way to avoid doing both is to speak and dance with people I *am* interested in." Aware her explanation came out a little sharp, she refocused her attention on Hunter and fixed a smile on her face. "Like you."

The corners of his mouth twitched, but if he was fighting a laugh, he managed to hold it back. "I'm honored to have made the cut, and under other circumstances I'd be happy to risk an ass-kicking to dance with a beautiful woman, but I'm expecting another beautiful woman to come through the door any second, and…well…I don't play games with her."

Damn. This guy might actually restore her faith in mankind. Without really meaning to, she relaxed in his arms. "Savannah mentioned something about you falling hard recently."

"Beau's got a big mouth," Hunter complained, but the easy grin made an encore.

"I doubt that." Her big sister's new husband fit the definition of the strong, silent type. "But Savannah's got a sixth sense about—"

A hand landed on Hunter's shoulder. "May I cut in?"

The voice held a deeper, more authoritative tone than she remembered, his Georgia drawl polished so smooth only a knowing ear would pick it up. All that *deep, smooth,* and *authoritative* made his question sound more like an inevitability than a request.

Hunter turned, and, in doing so, left her at the mercy of a determined green gaze. A gaze capable of luring her on an unwilling—and unwise—detour down memory lane. A gaze with the power to heat up her hormones, even after a decade, at the same time it fired her temper. The flash of satisfaction in those wicked depths told her the bastard had clocked her reaction from the other side of the room.

"That's up to the lady," Hunter replied, probably figuring one of them should respond.

Hell to the no. Shane might have put a tailored suit on his ridiculously impressive frame, and trimmed his thick, dark hair to a civilized length so it didn't fall like a raven's wing over his brow anymore, but she knew firsthand a dangerous heart beat beneath his respectable facade. She'd outgrown her bad-boy phase a long time ago. Been there. Done that. Got the scars to prove it. "No, thanks."

At her refusal, Hunter subtly shifted so she stood behind him, and she supposed she would have needed to get her estrogen checked if she hadn't experienced a small thrill watching two prime examples of the male animal silently square off. But after a moment, Shane merely shifted his attention to her, and—goddamn him—smiled. "What's the matter, Sinclair? Don't trust yourself in my arms?"

"Don't flatter yourself." She wasn't some love-struck schoolgirl, susceptible to eyes as captivating as trapiche emeralds, or lips seductive enough to make bullshit sound like gospel.

Those lips curved into the I-dare-you grin she blamed for some of her most regrettable decisions. She could hear his unspoken challenge from across the space separating them. From across oceans. Across time.

Don't fall for it…

"Fine. One dance. Then you leave." She wasn't falling for a damn thing. She was beating him at his own game—investing three minutes of her evening to get rid of him for the rest of her life. As soon as he took her hand, however, she knew she'd miscalculated. The single touch generated tiny sparks of recognition from every cell in her body. Before she could fully extinguish them, his arm closed around her waist and he pulled her against him. *All* the way against him, so her breasts rested against the unyielding expanse of his chest, and the big hand dominating the small of her back tipped her hips into the cradle of his. Hard thighs brushed hers.

"Sinclair, I can make a dance last all night."

She sensed, rather than saw, Hunter back off. A self-preserving part of her begged to do the same, but pride demanded she stay the course. Show Shane he didn't have the capacity to rattle her. Not even when he settled both hands low on her hips, in the kind of cocky, possessive gesture once guaranteed to send her pulse skyrocketing.

Different time. Different place. They'd both changed since then. She'd gotten wiser. He'd gotten a little taller, and a lot…manlier. His lean, youthful frame had solidified into hard-packed muscle, tense with leashed power everywhere it pressed against her. The once naturally smooth line of his jaw now looked like it saw a razor on a daily basis. Her inner thighs itched at the hint of five-o'clock shadow, and his lips kicked up a notch as if he'd read her mind.

Not in this lifetime. She lifted her chin and held up her end of the stare-down while couples circled around them. Somewhere up in the rafters, rotating fixtures showered the dance floor with a dizzying rain of lights, while Paul McCartney sang simple, eloquent words about friends, and lovers, and memories.

The edges of her vision grew blurry, and her world narrowed to him. Just him. The song, or the atmosphere… or *something*…made her feel lightheaded. Or maybe the sensation had to do with the fact that while she was holding his gaze, she was also holding her breath? She inhaled, sending much-needed air to her brain, as well as the completely unneeded scent of sophisticated cologne, along with a hint of something she hadn't had a whiff of in ten years, yet her memory instinctively recognized as Shane.

He leaned in close, so his breath tickled the sensitive skin along the side of her neck. "You're a terrible pen pal, baby girl."

Her? What a low and completely unfair blow, especially coming from *him*. He was a…a…whatever. She ignored the comment, and the old endearment, and concentrated on drawing a deep breath. She would hold her tongue, because calling him a jackass on the dance floor in the middle of her sister's wedding conveyed a message, all right, but not *You can't rattle me*. Ultimately, the past didn't matter. The present mattered. Most specifically, how long before she saw the last of him.

"What are you doing here?" The question came out snippier than she would have liked, but she couldn't help it. He was crowding her with his height and his muscles—the scent of his skin, the sound of his voice, and lot of banished memories.

"Celebrating the bonds of holy matrimony. Same as you."

"I don't mean *here*." She gestured around the reception, although how he'd ended up as someone's plus-one also mystified her. "I mean, what are you doing in Magnolia Grove?" A fair question, in her mind, because even though he'd been born and raised in this town, he hadn't set foot anywhere near the place for years. His parents had moved to Illinois shortly after he'd left for boot camp, and he hadn't kept in touch with anyone local—least of all her. As far as she was concerned, he didn't have any reason to be there.

"Maybe I've missed my hometown?"

"Try again. You hated everything about Magnolia Grove."

His hold on her tightened fractionally. "Not everything."

She refused to get drawn into a conversation about what he liked, or missed. A ten-year absence demonstrated pretty clearly how deep his feelings for the town and everyone in it ran. "Sentiment didn't pull you back, so I'm going to guess work."

"Would you believe me if I said both?"

She rolled her eyes, but his smile only widened. "The city requested bids for emergency planning services, and the firm I work for, Haggerty Consulting, won the contract."

This rang a bell. Magnolia Grove wasn't the small town it had been ten, or even five, years ago. The technology boom in nearby Norcross meant more residences and businesses in the surrounding areas, and Magnolia Grove definitely benefitted from the growth. Now a group of investors had plans to restore the Whitehall Plantation and turn it into a resort. To foster the project, the town council had agreed to create and implement a coordinated emergency response plan for the city, covering everything from fires to cyberattacks to natural disasters. "You're an emergency planning consultant?"

She already knew the answer. He'd left town, not dropped off the face of the planet. Tidbits about his life still made their way back to Magnolia Grove, whether she wanted to know them or not. She'd checked out his picture and profile more than once over the years, but she'd choke on her own tongue before she'd confess as much to him.

"I'm one of the best," he responded, and somehow managed to make the assertion sound matter-of-fact rather than boastful. "And since I already have a baseline familiarity with the area, Haggerty opted to send me."

"Lucky us." It was official. Fate hated her.

"Lucky all around," he countered, and leaned in again. "The mannerly response would be to welcome me home, Sinclair."

The low, teasing words gently mocked her. "Welcome home," she ground out. "When do you leave?"

His laugh caressed her ear. "Who said I was leaving? Maybe I'll stay. This is my home, after all."

No. Fucking. Way. Magnolia Grove was *hers*, dammit. He'd forfeited it ten years ago. "It's changed a lot since you've been gone. I doubt you'd—"

"I can see it's changed." Long fingers trespassed below the invisible line of decorum at the small of her back to very deliberately trace the curve of her hip. The move brought every nerve ending in the vicinity to attention, and she had a funny feeling he wasn't talking strictly about the town. "I have to admit, those changes are part of the allure. Show me around."

Uh-uh. She wasn't the Welcome Wagon, and he wasn't staying. If she had anything to say about it, he'd be gone before—

"Hot damn!" a voice blasted from the other side of the room. "There's a knock-down, drag-out fight in the parking lot."

Sinclair whirled to see who called out, while all around her, people rushed toward the exit. A few jostles and one stomped toe convinced her to step aside. She made her way to the perimeter of the dance floor. When she turned around, Shane had disappeared.

So much for him sticking around. And ironic, really, that he'd pull a fade in the face of a disturbance, because there'd been a time when he'd have been the first guy to wade in and throw a punch. Were it not for that mile-wide impulsive streak, and his misplaced protective instincts, they would never have known each other except in passing. She'd grown up in a nice, comfortable house in one of Magnolia Grove's most distinguished neighborhoods, while he'd been raised in a run-down rental in the old section of town. He'd been two years ahead of her in school, although showing up for the sake of district attendance expectations hadn't seemed high on his list of priorities.

But there had always been something about him...

Since *she* had no desire to run outside and watch a couple of over-served idiots roll around in the dirt, she slipped into the small room the venue had allowed them to use for gifts and checked in with the wedding planner to get a sense of when they'd be doing the garter and bouquet toss. People were filtering back into the reception by the time she returned, which meant whatever drama had unfolded in the parking lot was under control. She saw her mother seated at a round, linen-draped table, talking with a gray-haired woman. She approached, realizing too late that her mom shared the table with gossipy old Claudia Pinkerton. The look her mother shot her absolutely forbade her from bailing.

Resigned to her fate, she kissed Mrs. Pinkerton's plump cheek, and took the empty chair next to her mother.

"Sinclair, dear. You look pretty as a picture in that dress. The color matches your eyes."

She smoothed her hand over the fitted bodice of the strapless, midnight-blue satin. "Thanks. The credit for the dress choice goes to Savannah, although I did warn her things would get ugly if she stuck me in sea foam. What happened outside?"

"You don't know?" Mrs. Pinkerton scooted her chair closer to the table. "Heavens, I nearly passed out from fright. The best man's girlfriend's baby daddy showed up drunk or stoned or some such nonsense and tried to snatch the baby right out of her arms."

"Hunter's girlfriend? Holy sh…heck," she modified as her mom whacked her knee. "Is everyone okay?"

Mrs. Pinkerton nodded. "Hunter knocked him on his you-know-what and then threw him in the pond. Your dance partner fished him out and handed him off to Sheriff Kenner. Deputies took the whole mess down to the station so as not to ruin Beau and Savannah's day."

"Speaking of dance partners," her mom interrupted, "who *was* that boy you were dancing with? You two seemed awfully familiar, but I couldn't place him."

"That's Shane Maguire," Mrs. Pinkerton supplied, her expression as eager as her reply. "Remember him?"

"The same Shane Maguire who broke your grandson Ricky's nose their senior year of high school?"

Sinclair resisted the urge to leap to Shane's defense. Ricky had definitely had it coming, but the Pinkertons were influential in these parts, and thanks to the very loud, very public fit Ricky's parents had pitched, few people knew, or cared, about the underlying facts.

Mrs. Pinkerton nodded. "A lot of folks considered him a troublemaker, just like his brother, but I've always had a soft spot for the boy. By the looks of that dance, you do, too, Sinclair."

Her mother's keen blue eyes cut to her. "You don't say?"

"As a matter of fact, I don't." She intended to disabuse anyone of that notion right quick. "He's been gone for ages. I barely know him. I simply shared a dance with an old schoolmate. End of story. Hey, Dad," she greeted her father as he ambled up to their table. "I heard you started some trouble outside."

He stopped behind her chair, and rested his hands on her shoulders. "Me? Get real. I finished it, kiddo."

"Bill, please don't tell me you got involved—"

"Relax, dear." He winked at Sinclair and then turned his smile on his wife. "Kenner had everything under control by the time I came along. An impressive state of readiness, I have to say. Mayor Campbell credited the city's new consultant with the speedy response. Apparently he suggested they muster up some overtime budget so Kenner could increase patrols for things like weddings, since the combination of gathered family and host bar sometimes makes for interesting results."

"Well, good plan, as it turned out," her mother replied. "Did you get the present for Beau's parents while you were outside?"

Her dad's smile twisted into a quick frown. "Damn. No, I got so wrapped up in conversation with Campbell I forgot the whole reason I went out there in the first place." He dug his keys out of his pocket. "Back in a sec, ladies."

"I'll get it." Sinclair surged to her feet and snagged the keys. Better to fetch a bottle of champagne from her dad's car than stay at the table getting grilled over her dance with

Shane.

"It's behind the driver's seat," her father called after her. "Don't forget to lock up."

Sinclair tossed an A-okay sign over her shoulder and made her escape. The classic Mercedes 230 roadster was basically her father's third child. Even in twilight, the glossy red paint stood out against the backdrop of later-model vehicles. She worked her way toward it. Nobody loitered outside anymore, but her silver sandals slowed her down. The high, skinny heels sank into the grassy field that served as the parking area. Eventually she made it to the car and used the old-school key to unlock the door. A lever at the base of the seat tipped the seatback forward. She grabbed the gift bag containing the fancy champagne and returned the seat to its proper position. And if she rushed a bit more than normal, and caused the seat to fall back into place with a heavy thump, there was only one person to blame.

Shane.

She hadn't actually seen him leave, so it was possible he might be out here somewhere. She absolutely, positively didn't want to run into him in an empty parking area. Normally, she wasn't the kind of person who ran from a confrontation, but he'd had his dance, and she wasn't interested in extending the reunion. Staying on high alert spared her the trouble of telling him she had better things to do than play tour guide.

It took about three seconds to back out of the car and push the lock down. The wind kicked up as she turned away and slammed the door. Her sunk-in sandal heel prevented her from taking what she'd intended as a decisive stride toward the pre–Civil War cotton warehouse now enjoying a second life as an event venue. Before she managed a full step, a hard pull from behind stopped her short.

Uh-oh. With dawning dread, she turned to find the back of her dress trapped in the car door. Dammit. Impulse had her giving it a desperate tug, which accomplished nothing. *Don't panic. Just unlock the door, and…* Double dammit. Where were the keys?

The dread turned heavy and landed like a brick in her stomach. Her father's keys gleamed at her from exactly where she'd left them. On the seat of the car. The locked car. Her gaze automatically scanned the lot for help, but came up empty. Update. The keys were on the seat of the locked car, in the deserted parking lot.

Fuuuuck. She leaned against the door and stared up at the first twinkling stars. *You fed your skirt to the Benz, and now you're stuck here with your ass hanging out until somebody comes along. Just pray to God it's not—*

"I've been trained to spot risks, but even I didn't see this coming. Need some help, Sinclair?"

Chapter Two

Call him a masochist, but the way Sinclair tossed her long, dark hair over her shoulder and said, "No, thank you," in a voice capable of freezing the balls off Satan made him want to risk kissing the go-to-hell pout off her lips. Then again, he'd been battling the urge to kiss her since he'd arrived at the reception and gotten his first in-the-flesh glimpse of her in a decade.

Instead he crossed his arms and braced a hip against the engineering masterpiece currently holding her skirt hostage. A quick look through the window confirmed what he already suspected. "Locked the keys in the car, did we?"

"No *we*. It's not your problem." She moved the gift bag she held from her side to her chest, like a shield. In an effort to put some distance between them, she took a step away. The sound of a seam ripping stopped her retreat.

Words would be overkill. He simply raised an eyebrow.

"Pack up that look and take it somewhere else." She wrapped her fingers around the gold foil neck of the bottle in the gift bag, and pulled it free, holding it like a bat. "I can get myself out."

"A glass bottle makes a lousy key. You could get hurt." He took the champagne from her and slipped it back into the bag. "Let me help."

Her little nose went in the air. "I'm fine."

That she was. Even finer than he remembered, and his body still battled the consequences of having all that fineness pressed up against him. Of course, he remembered a girl—beautiful, headstrong, and out of his league in ways he'd been too much of a dumbass to fully appreciate at the time—but ultimately still a girl. Logically, he knew the same ten years that had transformed him from an eighteen-year-old fuckup to a VP of disaster planning and crisis management had turned her from a sixteen-year-old heartbreaker to a full-fledged adult. But the awareness hadn't prepared him for the power and glory of the woman. Nothing could have.

When he'd reluctantly accepted this assignment in his old hometown, he'd expected to see her again. Wanted to. For curiosity's sake, and old times' sake, but he hadn't expected to *want* her again. The strength of the reaction took him off guard—and not much did anymore. He shifted until he had her hemmed in between his body and the car, and watched her pupils expand to round, black islands in the stormy seas of her irises. The small, involuntary reaction sent him flashing back to humid nights alive with the sound of her hitching breaths, and those same dark pupils blown wide from everything he was doing to her. Everything they were doing to each other. He reached behind her and grabbed a fistful of her skirt, liking the jolt of lust he experienced at her quickly indrawn breath. He gave the skirt a testing tug.

"I don't know, baby girl. I'd say it's got you good. I could free you in less than five seconds, without putting so much as a scratch on you or the car, and the only thing I ask in return is for you to show me around."

"No deal. I'll handle it," she shot back and braced her free hand in the center of his chest.

He stayed put, letting the tension crackle between them. Chemistry notwithstanding, she very clearly wanted nothing to do with him. That fact had also caught him off guard. Her cool disdain brought out a remnant of his former self he thought he'd outgrown a long time ago—the impulsive kid who acted first and thought about the consequences later. Case in point? He shouldn't have said he was considering staying in Magnolia Grove. He wasn't. Haggerty had sent him to do a job. He intended to do it well and be on his way. If, in the process, he showed the haters in his hometown a Maguire boy had made something of himself, all the better. Returning permanently, however, was not part of the plan. But her eagerness to be rid of him had made him want to get under her skin.

Her current predicament only strengthened the urge. How had he forgotten her stubborn streak, or how entertaining it was to mess with her? "Okay, then." He backed off, and gave her a have-it-your-way shrug. "I'll leave you to it. No pressure, but I think the whole crowd is coming out soon for the bouquet toss." With that observation hanging in the air, he turned away and timed his steps to the silent countdown in his head...*three, two, one...*

"Okay. Wait."

He stopped, but didn't turn around. A man proceeded at his own risk when he pissed off a southern woman, and the smile of victory splitting his face would definitely piss her off. "Yes?"

"I'll accept your help. I'm sure it won't kill me to spend a couple hours playing tour guide."

A couple hours? Fuck no. He wanted more time with her, and he wasn't above negotiating to get it. He turned, regarded her calmly, and tossed her own words back to her. "No deal.

I've done some research, and I know at least a dozen new developments I need to check out firsthand. Twelve tours—I pick the destinations." Drawing on body language to tell her he wasn't dicking around, he folded his arms across his chest and stood his ground.

"Twelve…?" Her voice trailed off as she digested the demand, and he fought back another laugh when she stomped her foot. "Absolutely not."

He shrugged again, and started walking. Fortune favored the bold, because somewhere in the distance, a door slammed.

"Two tours," she countered, but he detected a distinct note of desperation in her voice.

"Six tours. Best and final."

The silence stretched so long he worried he'd overplayed his hand and she intended to call his bluff. Goddammit, he was going to have to give in and go pop the lock for nothing except his peace of mind. But then he heard her long, aggrieved sigh.

"Fine. Six tours. Not a mark on the car."

He turned and walked back to her. "Or you?"

Her chin came up as he drew near. "That goes without saying."

"Does it?" He dropped his gaze, and took a slow tour of some territory he'd once been intimately familiar with, starting at her bare shoulders and continuing to where satiny skin disappeared beneath blue silk. "I remember finding some extremely creative places to leave marks." He ran his finger along the neckline of her dress. "So you wouldn't get in trouble. You didn't need to be as cautious with me."

"I"—she broke off and swallowed—"I don't remember…"

Oh, yeah. She remembered. He took the gift bag out of her hand and set it on the roof of the Mercedes. "I'll let you in on a little secret, Sinclair."

"What?" The word barely qualified as a whisper.

"I'm still extremely creative." With that, he dropped to his knee, and peered behind her.

Her hand smacked his shoulder. "What are you doing?"

"Seeing if I can find a creative solution to your little predicament." The position gave him an up-close look at the tangle of her skirt in the car door, the torn seam that rendered the dress un-wearable—he turned his head slightly—*aaand* the tiny, lacy, black panties that left mouthwatering portions of her ass bare to his view. Without doing any sort of motive check, he let his cheek brush the smooth flesh.

Muscles quivered in response. The hand on his shoulder switched to the top of his head, but she didn't push him away. He trailed his lips across her thigh, automatically following the line of her panties where it hugged her hip and arrowed around front.

Her shuddery exhale triggered his inhale. Her scent stormed his senses, achingly familiar, and dangerously arousing. The molecules infiltrated his brain, coated the back of his throat, and left him dizzy from need. Balancing before her on both knees, taking a hip in each hand, he slowly closed in on the sheer triangle covering the prize.

"Shane…"

He took another hungry inhale. The tip of his nose skimmed the lace. "Yes?"

Those slim fingers slid down until her palm cupped the back of his head. Her thighs parted. "Ye—"

A car alarm shattered the silence and broke the spell lust and memories had woven around them. She jerked away, shoved her skirt down, and glared at him. "*That's* not part of our deal."

He stood, intentionally taking up the space she'd tried to carve out for herself. "Don't kid yourself, Sinclair. That's always been part of our deal." True, but the retort stemmed from pure frustration. With himself, for letting his dick take charge of things when the rest of him had just managed to gain a little headway, and with her, for trying to deny the pull between them.

"Our agreement involved you getting me out of this mess"—she poked his pectoral—"not inspecting my underwear. Can you do it, or not?"

He was reasonably confident he could do both. "Here." He shrugged out of his suit jacket and slung it around her shoulders.

"Thanks, but I—hey!"

His fingers found the zipper pull between her shoulder blades and whipped it down before she could finish her protest. As the dress pooled around her ankles, he hauled her against him and lifted her clear.

"This is your idea of a rescue?" Her voice pitched up with each word.

"You're free. The car's fine. I believe that satisfies the terms of our deal."

"Put. Me. Down."

"Yes, ma'am." He let her slide slowly down his body. Her eyes widened when his hard-on raked her stomach. As soon as her feet touched the ground, she backed away, but he saw her gaze dart to the front of his pants. She bit her lip and shifted her attention to some point over his shoulder.

"This hardly improves my situation."

That depended on the perspective. From his vantage point, things couldn't get much better. He drank in the sliver of skin on display between the edges of his jacket. The small rose of black silk perfectly centered in her lush cleavage, her flat stomach, the scrap of lace he'd come within a hairsbreadth of kissing just seconds ago. But the clatter of a door and the hollow sound of footfalls on porch boards heralded company, and he didn't want to share the view. He swept her into his arms. Her little huff of breath told him she hadn't anticipated the move. "Don't criticize. This is only phase one of the plan."

"Manhandling me is phase two?"

"Saving your sweet ass is phase two." He strode to the passenger side of his rented Range Rover, unlocked the doors, and deposited her inside. "Wait here."

A quick trip to the trunk of the SUV gained him what he sought, and a few strides later he offered her the USMC T-shirt and cut-off sweats he'd stowed in his gym bag. "Put these on. I'll take the gift inside, grab your things, and tell Savannah about your wardrobe malfunction. When I get back with your purse, you can drive home and change. If you hurry, you'll make it back in time to see the happy couple off."

Whatever argument she'd been preparing faltered in the face of his comprehensive planning—or maybe the thought of missing Beau and Savannah's departure. She took the clothes he held and spared him a "Thank you."

"I live to serve," he replied and left her to change while he saw to phase two. It didn't take long to find Savannah, offer up a vague explanation, and entrust her with the gift bag in exchange for her sister's purse.

When he returned to the parking area, Sinclair was already standing beside his car, looking ridiculously sexy with her slim body swimming in his shirt, and his sweat shorts riding low on her hips. It would take all of three seconds to rid her of those clothes. He imagined wrapping his fist around the T-shirt and tearing it off. The bra he'd glimpsed earlier would come next. The lacy, strapless confection pretty much begged to be stripped away. Images burned into his brain, and his palms tingled at the thought of holding her bare breasts, lifting them and lowering his head, seeing if they were as responsive as they'd been ten years ago when he'd been the first guy to touch them...kiss them...draw them into his mouth as deeply as he could and devour her until she buried her face in his hair to muffle her cries of pleasure.

His better judgment intruded. *Not tonight. Probably not*

ever, if you keep standing here, staring at her tits. He cleared his throat and handed her the purse. "I'll walk you to your car."

"That's not necessary." She opened the sleek, blue silk bag and pulled out her keys. "I've got it from here… Shoot. I locked my dad's keys in the car. I wonder if I'll be able to get a locksmith out this late on a Saturday?"

"And that brings me to phase three of the plan."

"There's a phase three?"

He took her hand and led her through the maze of parked cars to the Mercedes. "Phase three." While she watched, he withdrew the compact multi-tool he kept on his key chain, extended the lock-pick modification, and went to work. After a moment, he found the release. A twist, and the lock popped. He opened the door, retrieved the keys from the front seat, and handed them to her, along with her torn dress. "Anything else?"

Her eyes narrowed. "If you knew how to open the door all along, why the hell did you…?"

To hell with not pissing off a southern woman. He didn't even try to hold back his grin. "You negotiated for your freedom. You didn't specify I had to use the most expedient means available."

He heard her muttered curse before she turned on her heel and stormed off.

"Hey, Sinclair?"

"What?" She slowed but didn't bother stopping.

"I'm booking my first tour. Tomorrow afternoon. I'll pick you up."

Chapter Three

"*This* is your idea of a tourist attraction?"

Shane ignored Sinclair's incredulous tone and instead appreciated the sight of long legs encased in skinny jeans and black riding boots stepping down from the driver's seat of a silver Tahoe. Her slouchy red coat popped against the gray February sky. He pushed away from the flagpole he'd been leaning against as she crossed the empty parking lot. He'd lost the battle to pick her up—she'd claimed a tight schedule and insisted on meeting him—but he'd gotten her where he wanted her on a Sunday afternoon, and he considered that a victory.

"I never said tourist attractions." He steered her along the front of the building. "I said new developments."

She frowned and tapped the "1938" carved into the granite stone set into the corner of the brick structure. "The high school's been here forever, and given you managed to earn a diploma from this very institution, I assume you know your way around just fine without my help."

"I see lots of changes." He pointed to the buildings flanking the original schoolhouse. "Two new wings, a refurbished gymnasium, new football field and expanded grounds. C'mon. Let's look around."

"Thinking of trying out for the team? I hate to break it to you, but you missed your window of opportunity by about ten years."

"I wouldn't say I *missed* it. I had no interest in banging heads with a bunch of sweaty guys." He reached out and touched the articulated silver and crystal dragonfly pinned to the collar of her coat, making one iridescent wing flutter. "I had other interests. So did you, if I recall."

She took a step back and snuggled into her coat. "It's fair to say neither one of us has glory days to relive. What are we doing here, Shane?"

Oh, they had glory days, and he was more than happy to relive certain aspects, but the exasperation in her voice told him the better tactic right now would be to focus on the present. "Any comprehensive municipal disaster plan encompasses the schools, and identifying the optimal evacuation routes firsthand gives me a leg up on assessing the viability of their existing procedures."

All totally legit, but the chance to visit the place where they'd first met factored into his choice. Try as she might to keep a lock on the past, he figured nostalgia ultimately worked in his favor. They'd shared a lot, back in the day, caught up in each other with the kind of all-consuming intensity that made any risk seem reasonable, and any obstacle insignificant. The wildfire of emotion had probably been destined to flame out even if life hadn't gotten in their way, but seeing her again stirred the embers and made him realize he hadn't experienced anything close in a long time.

And he wanted to. Chalk it up to pure, simple lust, or the challenge of breaking through the wall of resistance he'd slammed into headfirst last night. And yes, also to reconcile the past and tie things off properly this time. He could still hear his former drill instructor—now his boss—telling him, *Son, consider her the one that got away, and move on.* He had, because there'd been no other option, but a small, persistent sense of unfinished business lingered in the back of his mind.

Her narrowed eyes conveyed skepticism. "I haven't participated in so much as a fire drill here since I graduated. Shouldn't you do this with someone who knows what's what?"

"I'll do that, too, eventually. This afternoon I just want to get the lay of the land, and I want company while I do it." To goad her into doing what he asked, he added, "Why the reluctance? I thought you were immune to me?"

"I'm totally immune to you. I'm just not a big fan of wasting time. But whatever." She lifted a shoulder and let it drop. "It's your time. Where do you want to start?"

"This way." He guided her around the main building and onto a concrete walkway that formed a border between the buildings and the sports fields.

She fell into step beside him. After a moment, manners got the best of her. "How's your family?"

"Predictably dysfunctional." The reply came out terser than he intended, and he didn't want to leave her with the impression he gave a shit over something he'd come to terms with a long time ago, so he elaborated. "Derek, as I expect everyone around here knows, is currently a guest of the good state of Alabama. He's about halfway through a three-year stint at Draper."

"I know." She laid a hand on his arm for a brief moment, and said, "I'm sorry."

The simple sympathy in her voice told him she might be one of the few people to actually mean the words. Though just three years apart, he felt like he hardly knew his older brother anymore. The first time Derek had gotten himself in real trouble—picked up by Atlanta PD for assault—Shane had only been fifteen. Even so, he'd heard all the whispers and seen the way people had looked at him like it was only a matter of time before he followed in his brother's footsteps. He very nearly had.

He shrugged. "Not his first time, probably not his last. He excels at bad decisions, and he won't listen to anybody, including me."

"I hope that changes." As she spoke, she crossed her arms and hunched her shoulders against the chilly breeze.

"Me, too, but I'm not holding my breath."

"And your folks? They're still in Illinois?"

"Mom works at a nursing home outside Chicago. Dad's doing as little as possible, as always."

Parenthood had come early and unexpectedly to Mandy and Gregory Maguire. The shotgun wedding arranged by her parents had stuck, but an exchange of rings didn't actually prepare a person for raising kids. He and Derek had run wild growing up. Acting out to get their parents' attention hadn't done anything except earn them bad reputations and ensure that in any situation requiring the benefit of the doubt, they wouldn't get it.

"You live in Chicago now, too?"

She phrased it as a question, but he detected a hint of deductive certainty in her voice.

"What makes you think so?"

She stopped and ran her hand down the sleeve of his green cashmere sweater until she reached the stainless-steel band of his Breitling chronograph. "Oh, please. You've got city all over you. A speck on the map like Magnolia Grove can't hold you now. It never could."

He liked her hand on him, even if her underlying intention was to push him away. Technically, she might be right, but he found himself playing devil's advocate just to keep her engaged. "I've been bouncing around the globe since I got my Eagle. I'm not rooted anywhere."

Even as he said the words, the crisp air, the scent of logs burning in a fireplace somewhere in the distance called up memories, as did the sight of her standing in the shadow of the old brick building. They knuckled through the foundations of the life he'd built since leaving Magnolia Grove, like a tree long gone but never properly excavated. Those useless remnants could still trip him up now and then if he didn't watch his step.

Maybe she read his mind, because she said, "You won't stay," and then turned and started walking again. "You couldn't get out of here fast enough, and once you left, you never looked back."

He followed, a little surprised at how ready he was to dispute her summary. She made it sound as if he'd left by his own choice and never contacted her again, which wasn't how things had gone down. "Seriously? That's the way you want to play it?"

"That's the way it was."

"I could argue your version of events."

"The past is the past. I don't want to talk about it." But her actions suggested otherwise, because she stopped and turned to him. "My only point is, you're not staying. Despite all the recent growth, this is still Magnolia Grove. It hasn't changed much from the place you walked away from." She glanced back at him. "And you haven't changed much from the guy who walked away. A job brought you back, nothing more."

Very true. A job had brought him back, and when he finished, he'd jump on a plane and head to the next. Which made her absolutely right, but he resented her words, and the certainty in her voice as she said them. He *had* changed, and for some pathetic reason, he wanted people to see that. The fact that she didn't hurt more than he liked to admit, so he spent a purposeful minute noting the potential bottlenecks in evacuation routes caused by the installation of several portable classrooms on one side of the quad. When he glanced at her again, he found her regarding him with a hard-to-quantify look on her face. "What?"

A smile flitted across her lips. "Nothing." She shook her head and took the path that cut across the quad, lined by a row of big, old maple trees. He measured his steps to hers and kept quiet—a strategy he'd always relied on when he wanted Sinclair to talk. Give her silence to fill.

The strategy still worked. After a moment, she laughed under her breath, and murmured, "Your job."

"My job is funny?"

"It's funny that the kid with a reputation for acting first and dealing with the shitstorm later now spends his time considering risks and implementing protective measures."

He shrugged. "I got tired of dealing with shitstorms— especially ones I should have been smart enough to prevent." Despite the offhand reply, pride expanded his chest. He'd left Magnolia Grove under the momentum of one of those self-induced shitstorms, well aware a lot of people assumed he'd never turn himself around. Coming back in a position of trust and authority felt good. The reluctant admiration in her eyes felt good.

"Preventing personal shitstorms is one thing. Preventing them for an entire city seems like a huge responsibility. That's a lot of people to protect." She slowed to run her fingers over the rough bark of a stark, leafless maple. The chilly air had turned her unpainted nails light blue.

He caught her hand and tucked it into the warmth of his and led them down the walkway toward the gymnasium. "I'm a protective guy."

That earned him a scoffing sound. "Ricky Pinkerton might beg to differ."

"See, we do have some glory days to relive," he teased.

Of course, they were standing in the shadow of the very spot where he'd broken Ricky's nose at senior prom, for not knowing the meaning of the word "no," despite Sinclair saying it more than once. He hadn't known her then, other than from a distance. A nice girl, from a good family, and on every guy's radar thanks to one of those truly remarkable growth spurts nature had bestowed over the summer. Ricky hadn't been the only one fantasizing about getting into her panties, but he'd definitely been the most aggressive in the face of a clear and unconditional refusal. "As it turns out, I wasn't protecting Ricky that night." He drew her to a stop. "I was protecting *you*."

She leaned back against the wall of the gym, and crossed her arms. Her chin came up, but her lips curved, and he knew what she was going to say before she said it. They'd been over this ground before. "Thank you, but I didn't need protecting. I had everything under control."

"Sure you did. I should have minded my own business."

Her stubborn little chin tipped higher. "I knew how to handle myself."

"Oh, yeah?" He faced her and braced one forearm against the building, to one side of her head.

Her gaze dropped to his mouth and then flicked up to meet his, and he fell into midnight blue.

"Yeah," she said softly.

He leaned in, bringing their faces close. "What if he'd done this?" Slowly, he slipped his hand inside her coat, under the loose hem of her sweater, and trailed his fingers around her naval.

"That wouldn't worry me."

Warm, cinnamon-infused breath washed over his chin. He inhaled, tasting her in the shared air, unlocking startlingly vivid memories of endless make-out sessions from their storage space somewhere deep inside his brain. Stolen hours spent behind the school, or down by the creek, or parked at the Lookout in his piece-of-shit truck, kissing until the windows fogged and their lips went raw. Need roused in his gut, heavy and staggeringly strong—like a hungry beast awaking after a long hibernation.

"How about this?" He eased his other arm around her, taking her weight against him as he pulled her close and slid his hand into the back of her jeans deep enough to tangle in her thong. "Would this worry you?"

Her breath caught. Slender hands grabbed his biceps and held on as he nudged his thigh between hers. She shifted until his pounding cock nestled against the fly of her jeans. "I'd tell him—"

"Me." He ran his mouth along the side of her neck, scoring her skin with the edge of his teeth. "What would you tell me?"

"Shane…"

Wait, his mind insisted, because that wasn't a yes, but his hands had a will of their own. One cupped her ass and hauled her more tightly against him. The other swept up her rib cage and closed over one soft, lace-covered breast. The tip tightened against his palm, and her little moan sent tiny vibrations all the way to his balls. He lifted his head and stared down at her and those plush, parted lips just millimeters from his.

"What would you tell me, Sinclair?"

. . .

Lips she hadn't kissed in years hovered enticingly close. Irresistible energy jumped the small distance and woke tiny nerve endings in hers, making them tingle with anticipation. No, not anticipation—that was too tame a word for the bone-deep need gripping her. Like a recovering alcoholic staring down a double shot of premium, ninety-proof whiskey, she could practically taste the illicit flavors flowing over her tongue, burning a path straight to her heart, and finally quenching a thirst she'd never completely cured with ten years of safe, harmless substitutes.

There'd been kisses before Shane—not many, and not memorable in any visceral way—and there'd been kisses since. Fun kisses, passionate kisses, a few surprises, but none had stormed her senses and captured her soul. None, except his. Would his kiss still affect her the same way after all this time, or was it some elusive magic generated by youth, fearlessness, and the utter newness of it all? More importantly, was curiosity a good enough reason to throw caution to the wind and find out?

"Shane," she whispered, and tipped her head a fraction of an inch, bringing their mouths closer. His breath warmed her lips. Rock-hard biceps flexed under her hands.

"Jesus, I missed you."

His drawl snuck into the low words and sent her heart bounding to close the distance forged by time and circumstances, but her mind pulled the leash. Hard. *Had* he missed her? Really? Where had he been during those weeks when her world had spun out of control? When she would have given anything for a single word? By the time he had finally reached out, it had been too late.

Way too late. Self-preserving instincts kicked in, jerking her back as far as the wall behind her would allow while she struggled to find her voice. It surfaced, weak and pitchy. "I'd tell you—"

"Tell me what you want," he murmured. "Anything." His fingers teased her aching breast while his lips brushed the corner of her mouth.

Her resolve wavered.

Stop. You went down this road before. It led to a long, hard fall, and some wounds that never healed. Don't let him draw you along the same dead-end path. Stay strong. It's only a matter of time before he leaves. "I'd tell you to back off."

Every muscle in his body pulled tight, like brake lines straining to stop a speeding truck. For half a second she thought—hoped—he wouldn't, but he dropped his head to her shoulder, and drew in a deep breath.

"Your call." He raised his head, and she got caught up in an unflinching green gaze. "But you know I would make it so good, Sinclair." He tugged gently on her nipple as he said her name, and she felt the pull of both in places she'd locked away years ago. Over her reluctant moan, he murmured, "Remember those nights we parked at the Lookout? I learned your body like a treasure map. I learned if I touched you here," he tugged her nipple again, harder, and another moan snuck out from low in her throat as heat twisted inside her, "you'd make that sound. And if I kissed you here," he feathered his fingers over her other breast, "your breathing would get fast and shallow. You'd wrap your arms around my head and hold onto me like your life depended on it, and I'd bite and lick and suck those gorgeous tits of yours while you straddled my lap and got the both of us so wet. Remember?" The hand in the back of her jeans edged around the waistband of her underwear. "Your panties would be drenched." He slid his fingers down the front of her jeans. "I'd be so hard it hurt, and you'd be so sensitive, as soon as I so much as grazed your little—"

"*Shane.*" Even she couldn't tell if that was an invitation or a warning. His fingers paused, but his voice continued stroking her need.

"Are you wet now? If I touched you, would you come in your panties for me, just like back then? I bet you would."

She damn well would, and the awareness was enough to scare her into putting the brakes on for real. "*Shane.*" She gripped his wrist, but didn't quite rouse the determination to drag his hand out of her jeans.

"Not so immune to me, are you?" The corner of his mouth lifted, but something hungry burned in his eyes.

He looked smug and dangerous, and the combination lit the fuse on her temper. She brought her knee up until it menaced his balls. "Want to find out?"

"Careful." One dark brow winged up. "That used to be your favorite toy, baby girl. You never know when you might want to play with it again."

If he expected her to laugh at the old joke, he was going to be sorely disappointed. She shoved him away. "I've outgrown it. You honestly think you can waltz into town and pick up where you left off?" Anger propelled her. She turned and started walking back the way they'd come, but after a few steps she stopped and swung around to add, "I hate to shatter your ego, Shane, but I haven't been sitting around waiting for you to come back and toy with me."

Dark brows lowered over flashing eyes. "You're involved with someone."

Okay, no. You do not get a secret thrill out of that possessive look. "I'm involved with my life. With my work, my home, my family —"

"Not a man." His expression cleared.

"You're not hearing me, Shane."

"I heard every word. You've got work, and a home, and your family. I want to know about all of it. Wednesday at five thirty. I'll pick you up."

She opened her mouth to tell him no, but he cocked a brow and kept on talking. "Or are you backing out of our deal?"

Pride took control of her voice. "I'm not backing out of anything." Then she spun on her heel and stomped away rather than face his "I win" smirk.

Dammit.

Chapter Four

Tiny leaves from the canopy of willow limbs overhead spiraled down in a lazy breeze. Sinclair tipped her head up to let the faint stirring of air cool her face. The sweet, fruity taste of Arbor Mist sangria lingered on her tongue, along with a hotter, smoother, far more addictive taste. Both made the view above her spin just a little. She definitely didn't need any more sangria, but she never seemed to get enough of Shane.

His fast, reckless mouth moved up her throat while maddeningly careful fingers stroked between her thighs. His touch lit up every cell in her body. His kisses set her on fire until she glowed white-hot. The intensity in his stormy green eyes quickened her heart. Made her feel wild and invincible. She sank her hands into his hair—thick and soft and in need of a trim—dug her knees into the fleece blanket she'd brought to cushion them from the packed earth within the curtain of the willow, and plastered her trembling body against his lean, hard, surprisingly powerful one.

"Please," she whispered. She was his in every way except this, and time was running out. To urge him on, she snuck her

hand between their bodies and wrapped her fingers around a part of him she'd explored to her heart's content with her hands, lips, and mouth over the last few weeks. The thick, hard length pulsed in her grip—reassuring and intimidating at the same time.

He groaned, and raised his head to look at her. A flush tinged his cheeks and did fluttery things to her stomach. His nostrils flared as he inhaled. "Sin…"

Whatever he was going to say faded into the humid evening air as she dragged her fist up, tugging velvety skin over a core of smooth steel. His flush deepened. His eyelids battled gravity for a moment, but ultimately his long, dark lashes fell, casting shadowy wings across his cheeks. Another, deeper groan rumbled up from his chest. "Uh-oh. Baby girl's found her favorite toy."

So true. She loved touching him—everywhere—but especially here. How could she resist such a fascinating set of contradictions? Strong, but vulnerable. Hard, but fragile.

Big.

Maybe bigger than anything nature intended for her to accommodate? The imposing shaft surged to new dimensions as she stroked, and her courage flagged a little.

As if he read her mind, he cupped her head and tipped her face to his. Labored breaths fanned her cheek. The strength in his hands, the sheer power of his body might have scared her, because she was about to put herself at the mercy of all that strength and power, but the way he banked it for her, and looked at her as if she was the most important thing in the world, chased away the fear.

He swept hair back from her sweaty temples and held her gaze. "You can play with me all night. Just like this. I guarantee it will be the best birthday of my life." Lips caressed her temple, and one of his hands swept down their bodies to cover her fist where it held him. "It already is."

The glint of the infinity symbol on his wrist caught her eye. She'd shaped the platinum wire herself and woven it into the black leather bracelet—a birthday present she'd made especially for him. She'd cut her thumb on a pointy sliver of wire in the process. The pain had been a fleeting thing, and worth enduring in order to give him something so heartfelt. The rest of his gift fell into the same category—one moment of pain to give him something special. Something she could only give once, and she needed to give it to him. Now. Besides, at this point, the torture of holding back far outweighed anything physical she might have to withstand.

"Your birthday is about to get better." Clinging to her bravery, she tightened her grip and angled his hard-on so it pointed her way. Before he could recover from the move, she lowered herself.

The wide, smooth head of his dick slid around for a second, feeling big and unwieldy in the comparatively small crevice she was trying to guide him through, but then, miraculously, she found the target, and pushed him in as far as she could before her tight muscles begged her to stop. She bit her lip to stifle a moan.

"Oh, Jesus." His hand flew to her hip, fingers digging into her skin. The other maintained a hold on the base of his cock. "Let me…let me…"

"Don't move," she managed, and heard the waver in her voice over the rush of blood in her ears. She barely felt his other hand move to support her trembling thigh. The stinging pain between her legs demanded all of her attention. She switched from holding him, to holding herself, her fingers forming a wide "v" around the place where their bodies connected.

Eyes closed, she gritted her teeth, and lowered herself a little more. The ache intensified to something impossible to get beyond. Tears burned. A million frozen needles pricked her skin, making her shiver, leaving her cold everywhere except the one spot where scalding heat refused to abate. "Are—are you in?"

"Baby girl, I'm about halfway there." His thumb swept over her trembling lip. "You're hurting."

Stoicism abandoned her. She nodded. "Bad."

"Want to stop?"

The clipped words told her the offer cost him. She blinked her eyes open and took in his tense jaw, the little notch between his brows, and his gaze locked on her face. "Does it feel good to you?"

A muscle in his jaw twitched. "No… Fuck." He dropped his chin to his chest, and groaned. "God yes. Being inside you feels like heaven."

All her emotions threatened to break loose. Holding them back inflicted a different type of pain.

The torture of holding back.

She'd put herself between a rock and a hard place, and there was only one way out. "Okay." She sniffed back tears and held him tighter to stop the shakes rattling her. "Okay. You do it. You've done this before."

"I've had sex before. I haven't done this *before. I don't want to hurt you."*

"Just do it fast."

"Sinclair…"

"Please?" Her teeth chattered over the word. "I trust you—"

He drew her back, and kissed her, hard. Then her world tipped on its axis, and she landed flat on her back on the blanket in a move controlled solely and exclusively by him. He kept right on kissing her while he hitched her leg up to his waist. The position, and simple physics, accomplished the deed in one searing second. He sank deep, tearing past her body's fragile resistance, swallowing her gasp as if by sealing his lips to hers he could absorb the hurt. When her cry subsided to a whimper, and the pain subsided—thank you God—to something hot and…itchy, he relinquished her mouth and trailed his lips over her cheek to kiss away tears she hadn't realized had snuck from beneath her closed eyes.

She forced them open, and drank in every beautiful plane and angle of his face, from the slope of his forehead, to the subtle hollows under his cheekbones, to his chiseled chin. "Happy birthday, Shane." Then she followed a need too consuming to fight and rocked her hips.

A shudder wracked his body. His pupils expanded, turning his eyes dark as they stared into hers. "I love you, Sinclair," he whispered.

The dam on her own emotions broke, and she let the words that had been building for the last three weeks tumble from her lips. "I love you, too. I love you…I love you…"

Even as she locked her arms around his shoulders and held on with everything she had, she couldn't protect the moment. Harsh light began to filter through the network of leaves above her. It burned through everything, like film caught in a projector, obliterating the sheltering tree, the warm night, and Shane.

Dread poured into her gut, heavy and sickening, as the light separated into shapes, and then the shapes fell into focus. Serious faces peered down at her from behind white surgical masks. New pain struck, low, unrelenting, and terrifying.

She tried to cry out, but her voice was a cloud—insubstantial and beyond her reach. Everything around her kaleidoscoped, and when the whirling stopped, she was lying in a hospital bed while her father—the man who had patiently assembled a thousand Barbie accessories for her and Savannah, coached their softball teams, and given her a silver chain and heart bracelet on her last birthday because he wanted to be the first man to give her jewelry—stared at her with a look of fury and desperation on his face she'd never seen before, and never *wanted to see again.*

"My sixteen-year-old daughter is lying in a hospital bed, and some fucking criminal is walking around scot-free. Give me his name, Sinclair. Give me his name or I swear to God, you're going to be grounded for real. No phone, no computer, no nothing…"

The churn of tires on gravel threw her out of the dream. She jerked upright in her chair, dragging in air like a drowning woman, scanning her surroundings through a blur of tears to reassure herself she was in the here and now.

The old boards of the barn she called home stared back at her, steady and reassuring. They'd withstood more than a century of challenges and done what they were supposed to do. Accepting the silent inspiration they offered, she wiped her face, pushed back from her worn-but-sturdy pine table, and headed to the door. She could handle half a dozen encounters with Shane Maguire.

She stepped outside, lowered her black sunglasses over her tired eyes, and slid the heavy barn door closed behind her. Shane killed his engine a moment before it clattered into place, making the noise sound all the more profound and final in the sudden silence. She turned in time to watch him climb down from the Range Rover. A civilized white button-down only emphasized the breadth of his shoulders and skimmed the trim lines of his torso before disappearing into tailored gray suit pants. With the shirtsleeves rolled up his forearms, his light-blue tie loosened, and two buttons at his throat hanging open, he looked like he'd just taken over the world and was ready for the next conquest. Then his focus landed on her, and his mouth curled up at one corner. He didn't say a word, but every step he took to close the distance between them told her he had his next conquest in sight.

Clear, green eyes took in her long, black V-neck sweater and leggings. Yes, her favorite sapphire teardrops dangled from her ears—the ones she knew set off her eyes—but she was a jewelry designer, for Christ's sake, and she'd be naked without at least one statement piece. She certainly hadn't dressed up for him, and if he didn't like it, he could just turn tail and be on his way, because she was damn tired. Two overheated, uncomfortable nights spent tossing in her bed, fighting off old memories, and new memories—it was *his* fault she couldn't sit at her kitchen table for five quiet minutes without falling asleep.

Irritation propelled her down the slight slope of her yard toward the drive. He met her halfway. Before he could say a word, she cut him off. "Just so we're clear, I'm not going to sleep with you."

• • •

"Been thinking about sleeping with me, Sinclair?"

Because he couldn't resist touching her, even with do-not-touch coming off her in waves, he slid her dark glasses up to the top of her head. The move disturbed her earrings. The dangling gems swung back and forth, sparkling in the afternoon light. She shivered, and he had a quick, dirty fantasy about making those eye-catching earrings dance to the rhythm of his body driving into hers, accompanied by the music of her husky voice breaking over his name.

"No." Eyes even bluer than the sapphires regarded him. "I'm thinking about not sleeping with you. And I have to be home by eight, so if this outing is an attempt at seduction, you're wasting your time."

He risked another brush of the earring, letting his fingertip skim her earlobe this time. "Our outing is my attempt to get reacquainted with my hometown. I can't be blamed if you find me seductive."

"I don't." She stepped out of his reach and put her sunglasses back on. "Not in the least."

"Well, then"—he gestured toward his SUV—"you have nothing to worry about, do you?"

Ready to prove the point to both of them, she swept past and headed to the Range Rover. He beat her there and opened the door for her. The stern look she shot him pulled a genuine laugh from his chest. "What? Holding the door constitutes seduction? If that's true, I attempted to bag an eighty-year-old woman at city hall this afternoon."

She climbed into the Rover, but not before he saw her lips twitch. "Shot down by a senior citizen?"

"Apparently." Satisfied he'd defused her mood, at least enough to get the small laugh, he shut the door and walked around the front of the car to the driver's seat. Once he got in, he paused to remove his tie. While he folded it, he eyed the barn. Weathered boards sat on a ballast stone and mortar base. One no doubt built by hand over a century ago.

"Rustic."

The dry observation earned him another laugh. He tucked his tie into the compartment between the seats and watched as she cast the old structure a fond look. "A couple years ago, Mrs. Pinkerton overheard me talking real estate with Mayor Campbell's wife. I mentioned I was looking for a place off the beaten track, with more privacy and personality than one of the cookie-cutter condos springing up around town. I needed lots of room, and light, as I wanted to include my workshop under the same roof. She jokingly suggested this place, but as soon as I saw it, I stopped laughing. I loved the potential of all the raw, open space, and the lack of pretense. It was built to be useful, and by God, I could use it. I went back to Mrs. Pinkerton and asked if she was serious. When it comes to money, she always is, so we worked out a deal."

"How much did she pay you to take a dilapidated barn off her hands?"

"Ha. Ha. You are funny. Needless to say, the price was right, which helped because it left me some cash for improvements."

"Improvements? I'm looking at the *improved* version?"

"Not fully. It's a work in progress, but I've done a few things, here and there—turned the loft openings into windows and added skylights. I've got more planned, but nothing that changes the fundamental character much. Not to get too new age-y about things, but the creative energy of the place is good."

"Yeah?" He inspected the barn again. "Is creative energy another way to say lack of plumbing?"

"Don't judge, princess. I have hot running water, flush toilets, and everything."

"All the comforts of home?" He didn't bother hiding the curiosity in his voice, hoping she might invite him in and show him around. And not just for the obvious reason that the tour could end in her bedroom. Her words from yesterday still rang in his mind. *I'm involved with life. My home, my family, my work.* He wanted to know about her life, but asking her straight out to share would only backfire. Dark glasses and folded arms spoke volumes. She had her barriers in place. She might be civil as long as he didn't do anything to threaten them, but she intended to keep him at a distance. Too bad for her he'd spent the last decade learning how to get around barriers, quickly and deftly, so the target never even realized defenses had been breached.

"All the comforts I need, for now," she conceded, "plus a very short commute down a flight of stairs to my studio."

Her body angled toward his, and he inwardly smiled. The conversation drew her in, whether she realized it or not. He lifted his hand from its perch along the seatback and touched her earring again. "Seems a little risky, keeping things like this lying around a barn."

Her perfume, or shampoo…something faintly floral… permeated the leathery new-car smell of the Rover. It made him want to drag her close and find out if the scent grew stronger when he buried his face in her long, unbound hair, or when he pressed kisses against the warm pulse at the base of throat. Or warm pulses in other places.

"Skylights and windows weren't my only improvements," she said, cutting into his rogue thoughts. "I installed a two-thousand-pound, fireproof, bulletproof, tamper-resistant safe, plus a top-rated alarm system wired for every entry point, including the skylights. Don't be fooled by appearances." She tapped the window with her fingernail. "That barn is both sanctuary and fortress."

Sanctuary. Fortress. Interesting terms. Sanctuary suggested she wasn't inviting him in anytime soon. He started the car and began backing down her narrow, unpaved drive. Fortress probably meant the building was secure enough for her insurance company, which wasn't a bad standard, but all that aside, he still had a hard time reconciling the girl who'd grown up ensconced in the comfort of one of the best neighborhoods in Magnolia Grove with the woman who lived a good two miles from her nearest neighbor, in a building originally meant for livestock and storage. Then again, she'd always had a soft spot for rough-edged things in need of attention. He'd qualified, once upon a time.

"So, it's livable?"

"Depends on whom you ask," she conceded, turning to check for cars as he approached the road and then giving him an "all clear" sign. "My mom keeps waiting for me to move into a 'normal' house, but she might change her tune once I'm done remodeling."

He pulled out onto the empty road and shifted to drive. "And where are you at with that?"

"The waiting stage. I need the city planning commission to approve my permits." The toe of her black boot—sexy, suede ankle boots today—bounced up and down, telegraphing her impatience with the process.

"I commandeered an office at city hall for the duration of the project. Want me to check on the application next time I'm there? I might be able to grease the skids for you."

The offer hung in the air. He kept his eyes on the road, veering left to take the route that wound north, but he felt her regarding him. He could practically hear the thoughts forming in her head. Shane Maguire, notorious fuckup, now regularly interacted with city officials. The mayor had him on speed dial. He worked on the right side of the line nowadays, and he got shit done.

"No worries," she finally replied and looked out the window at the trees zipping past. "I filed the application a couple weeks ago, just missing the deadline to get on the agenda for this month's meeting. There could be some back-and-forth with the plans. I doubt you'll be around long enough to see them through the entire review process."

Probably not. His calendar showed him in Seattle as soon as he finished here, and then on to the next client, and the next. Travel was an integral part of his job, and he liked it that way.

He didn't, however, like dismissals, and he recognized one when he heard it. His pride fought back. "What makes you assume I'm not still thinking about sticking around?" Technically, it wasn't a lie. He was thinking about it. Rejecting the thought, but still…

She continued staring straight ahead but pulled her mouth into an off-center frown. An immediate desire to sink his teeth into her upper lip shot through him. He could almost hear her little moan of pleasure. Almost feel her mouth go soft and seeking under his.

Could be he was thinking too loud, because she turned and caught him looking. Pink seeped into her cheeks. She dipped her head, and even with her eyes shielded by the glasses, he knew her gaze landed in his lap. His hard-on surged as if she'd actually touched him, and now his own groan threatened to fill the car.

"You're not sticking around," she said under her breath, then crossed her legs tight enough to hook her instep around her calf, and resumed staring out the window.

He turned his attention to the road, which grew windier as it climbed. A few seconds later, a hissing breath came from beside him. Sinclair shoved the glasses up and whipped her head around. Blue eyes narrowed on him. "Where are we going?"

"Tomochichi Lookout."

Her back went up. "I'm not going to the Lookout with you."

He reached across the console to gently pinch her arm, and then pointed to the WELCOME TO TOMOCHICHI LOOKOUT sign coming up on her side of the road. "I don't know. Kinda seems like you are."

"I mean," she ground out in a tone fueled by exasperation, "I didn't agree to go to the Lookout with you."

He'd expected her objections, and prepared for them. "You agreed to six tours of my choice. What's the issue, Sinclair? You always loved this place." True enough. A decade ago, they'd put in quality time at the Lookout. Many hours spent barely noticing the legendary view. They'd been too busy focusing on each other—on the duel of tongues, the slide of skin against skin, her breathless little whimpers when he kissed the right spot, and his ragged curses when she used her curious and oh-so-daring mouth on him.

"You told me you wanted to see the new developments. The Lookout has been here since…I don't know…the last ice age." She folded her arms and glared at him as he slowed the Rover to a stop. The windshield framed a postcard-worthy panorama of the sun hanging low over the valley. "There's no reason for us to be here."

"I told you I wanted to get the lay of the land." So saying, he unlatched his seat belt and tipped his head toward the view. "Can't think of a better way than from here." He deliberately waited a beat. "Unless you'd rather stay in the car?"

She got out, slamming the door hard enough to scatter a couple of squirrels and send them to the shelter of a high-limbed pine. He approached the low stone wall protecting the drop-off and kept tabs on her from the corner of his eye. She wrapped her arms around herself and focused on the view.

Hard not to. The endless, cloud-streaked sky tinged orange by the setting sun commanded attention, as did the expansive green valley cradling their town. After a few moments, she took a few steps closer, until she stood even with him. Well, more or less even. She left a foot of buffer between them.

"I haven't been here in ages. I'd forgotten how much you can see," she said, her voice hushed even though they were the only people around. "Those two subdivisions are new." She pointed to the tidy square parcels that would have been woods last time they'd shared this view. "And the community college. Oh, there's the Whitehall Plantation."

He nodded and mentally overlaid the resort plans on the landscape. The developers intended to incorporate the historic main house into the hotel. An additional building would be constructed for the obligatory full-service spa, as well as an indoor pool. The outdoor pool would overlook a world-class golf course—thirty-six holes strategically planted on gently rolling former cotton fields bisected by the Tomochichi Creek.

His eyes followed the line of the creek where it cut

across the property, and a thought struck. More to himself, he murmured, "That's a flood fringe."

"What? For the creek?" She stepped closer and peered down at the area in question. "The creek's never flooded, as far as I can remember."

"I'm sure it swells from time to time, but right now there's a natural overflow basin of unperturbed land, so no harm, no foul. If they install the golf course as planned, they're going to want to build up the creek banks rather than chance flooding their five-million-dollar investment every time it rains."

She arched a brow at him. "Is fortifying the banks a problem?"

He shrugged. "A little more engineering. Time and money. Nothing major."

They stared at their town for another long moment, watching lavender shadows blanket the valley as the glowing fringes of daylight disappeared behind the foggy blue peaks in the distance. Dry leaves crackled softly underfoot as she turned to him and sighed.

"Be honest, city boy. Do you really see anything here that captures your interest?"

He looked at her—straight into her eyes—just long enough to give her an answer, and let her back away if that's what she wanted to do.

She didn't back away, thank God. Wide eyes locked on him as he trespassed into her personal space. And then he was pulling her into his arms, and she was lifting up onto her toes, and their lips collided.

Ten years disappeared in one blinding instant. The feel of her, the taste—so sweetly familiar it nearly fractured his heart, but also intoxicatingly different. Stronger. Deeper. Hotter.

A needy sound came from the back of her throat. He pulled her closer, so she couldn't miss the fact that the need was mutual. Hands flattened against his chest, but she didn't push him away. She leaned in, opening her lips to allow his tongue access to every part of her mouth.

He reacquainted himself in a series of fast, hungry sweeps and long, deep plunges, desperate to devour everything at once like a starving man at a feast. Manners finally kicked in when she moaned again, this time a little desperately. He forced himself to slow down. Let her have oxygen. But she closed those plush lips around his tongue, applying suction as he withdrew, and he felt the pull all the way to the base of his cock. It slowed him down considerably. When he eventually lifted his head, they were both breathing heavy. He waited until she blinked her eyes open and focused on him.

"Does that answer your question?"

"What question?"

He laughed, despite the brutal pressure in his balls. "You wanted honest, Sinclair. I can't be more honest than this. Your turn."

Her gaze dropped to his mouth. She dragged her lip between her teeth, worrying the soft pink flesh until he thought he'd pass out from the blowjob those lips were giving him in his mind. But her eyes—they were the eyes of a woman at war with herself. So much so, she backed up a step, letting the cool air get between them. "What if I say I meant what I told you before, about how I'm not going to sleep with you?"

I'd say you're lying to both of us. But she wanted the lie, for now, and he played by her rules. Always. Which didn't mean they couldn't still play. He put his hands in his pockets and shot her a grin. "Slow your roll, baby girl. Last time I checked, there was a lot of road between all and nothing. And for us, the Lookout was always about the journey."

Chapter Five

For us, the Lookout was always about the journey.

The words echoed around Sinclair. Shane stood against the dramatic sky in his respectable white shirt and suit pants, with his hands in his pockets as if to suggest he posed no risk. No risk? Ha. The confident grin, the gleam in his eyes, and the assembly of hard, vital muscles covered by the facade of professional clothes told a different story. He was the very definition of risky. He always had been.

And yet, damn her, she was tempted to take the journey. His mouth on hers produced a complicated set of responses—a shockingly strong rush of desire. Curiosity. Caution, because old feelings left a painful weight in her chest, as if she'd swallowed too much of something. God only knew what was going on in her head. More than she could unpack right here and now, so she took another step back and gave him a deliberately obtuse answer. "What journey? We both know where this road ends." He could interpret that any way he chose.

"You have a terrible memory." He strode to the passenger

side of the Rover and opened the door for her. "Get in, and I'll refresh it for you."

How should she interpret that? It wasn't lost on her that he'd shifted the burden of clarifying things back to her. She walked over, her strides unhurried, but her mind raced back to another time—a time when the sight of him standing by his truck would send her shimmying down the tree outside her bedroom window, hurrying across the moonlit front yard, and flinging herself into his waiting arms.

She didn't do that kind of reckless abandon anymore. These days she walked into things with her eyes open, and always, always, with a clear path for how she intended to walk out.

Maybe tonight wasn't so different? She could walk in easily enough. No explanations necessary, and nobody had to know. He'd take care of the exit. Despite what he said, she had no doubt about that. Only one uncertainty remained. Sex was off the table, so exactly what was she walking into?

The flash of his smile dared her to find out, and she'd never been one to back down from a dare. Gathering every ounce of calm at her disposal, she stepped up into the SUV and settled herself in the passenger seat. He closed the door, came around, and climbed into the driver's seat. And then, for a long moment, he just faced forward. She followed his gaze out the window. Lights in the valley below twinkled to life in the unfurling dusk. The top corner of the crescent moon shone from above a fringe of pine tops. Somewhere in the distance, an owl hooted.

The call seemed to spur him into action. Nature hadn't been the soundtrack of their nights at the Lookout. He hit the button on the dash to fire up the battery, and then tuned the radio until he found a station. Sam Hunt flowed from the speakers and warned some unnamed girl he was going to make her miss him.

Shane turned to her, relaxed as could be with one arm braced against the steering wheel and the other resting on the back of the seat. Slowly, as if he had all the time in the world, he leaned in and kissed her again. "Remember now?"

Of course she remembered. She remembered kisses so long and deep and melding she felt as if they'd absorbed each other. She remembered yearning to be even closer. Crawling into his lap to make it happen, and sighing with gratitude when he'd undone her blouse, peeled her bra away, and touched her breasts. He'd been the first boy to see them, much less handle them, but he'd been so reverently gentle, and then so exquisitely rough, her body still reacted whenever she thought of it.

Another night, his hands had gone on to bring her another first. This one so overwhelming he'd had to muffle her bewildered cries of pleasure. And that had only been the beginning. His mouth…those patient lips and that tireless tongue, had driven her beyond pleasure. They'd introduced her to desperation right before they'd introduced her to an orgasm so shattering it had reduced her to tears. One of many. Nobody had ever made her lose herself the way he did.

Would he still? Her heart pounded hard at the prospect, but glancing around the burled wood and hand-stitched leather interior of the Rover offered a big, bracing dose of reality. They definitely weren't kids anymore, and letting a guy get to third base in a car was the kind of insanity reserved for sixteen-year-old girls who didn't know what the fuck they were doing. "Are you serious? I'm twenty-six years old."

"Is there an age limit on vehicular necking?"

"We did a hell of a lot more than neck."

His smile turned downright triumphant. "See?" He leaned over and nuzzled her ear. "It's coming back to you."

Clean, expensive cologne teased her nose at the same time his lips teased her skin. "I'd do this…" He eased his body closer, surrounding her until he could run his thumb up and down her arm, brushing the swell of her breast in the process.

Under her sweater, nerve endings tingled. Muscles in her abdomen tightened as heat centered there and then seeped lower. She squirmed in her seat. "That was a long time ago. We're both experienced adults, and adults don't do this. It's more all-or-nothing after a certain age."

"Not tonight." He switched his hold to the back of her neck and kissed the line of her jaw. "Tonight, we get reacquainted with everything in between. Starting here…" He covered her mouth with his and delivered another kiss— the kind of long, persuasive kiss that took what was offered and asked for more at the same time. The kind of kiss that said nothing was a foregone conclusion, because every moment was a destination unto itself.

The kind of kiss she could never resist. She dug her fingers into his shoulders, and kissed him back. He used his lips to part hers, but then her tongue set its own agenda, racing along the edge of his teeth until he bit down, deliberately trapping it. Other parts of her body tingled in anticipation of the same treatment. His taste filled her mouth. Past and present blurred while she drank him in.

Long, suspended moments passed while his mouth moved over hers. Eventually, he eased back just enough to let her breathe, but his hand at the back of her neck kept her close. So close their lips stayed in contact while she dragged in a lungful of oxygen. The touch-and-go brush of his mouth against her kiss-dampened lips took her back in time, while simultaneously holding her firmly in the moment.

They'd left "nothing" in the dust as soon as he'd pulled into her drive. She'd taken "all" off the table before she'd gotten in his car and figured that would be that, but he was proving her wrong. And she didn't want him to stop.

He knew it. He sank his teeth into her lower lip, trapping

it, bestowing a quick, hard bite and not bothering to hold back a growl of satisfaction when she grabbed two handfuls of his shirt front and silently begged for more. He gave her more, doling out similar treatment to her upper lip. A hungry sound snuck past her throat to reverberate around the confines of the car and brought his mouth slamming down on hers with renewed urgency. Need ignited her blood. She couldn't keep still. Their kisses grew faster, hungrier, far less precise.

He skimmed his hand under her sweater and along her spine. Fingers followed the line of her bra, a question inherent in the touch.

Yes, some wild part of her responded immediately. She arched closer, hoping the gesture would be all the discussion required.

"Use your words, baby girl." He traced the elastic again.

"Goddammit," she muttered between kisses. She wanted more of this—the heat and the rush. What she definitely didn't want was for him to say or do anything to slow things down and give her time to reconsider. Going with impulse, she tightened her hold on the front of his shirt and yanked.

Buttons ricocheted against the dash, and the fabric gaped to the middle of his chest.

"I'll take that as a yes," he rasped. His hands came up to cover hers, stilling them as she prepared to take a second tug. Quickly, he pulled his shirttails free of his pants. "Go on. Do your worst."

Her second effort got the job done, but she didn't spare a moment on the accomplishment. She claimed her reward, running her palms over the hard expanse of smooth, warm skin. She didn't know where to touch first but found herself visiting familiar highlights like the lines of his collarbones and the shallow channel between his pecs. She lingered there, spreading her fingers and raking her nails through the dusting of hair now shading his chest. Would it tickle her lips?

Her breasts? Before she could contemplate the questions too deeply, her hands discovered other terrain and veered downward to learn every irresistible contour of his abs. They rippled under her touch, and her mouth went dry.

"My turn," he growled and slid both hands under her sweater. The wool bunched up as he bracketed her rib cage. His fingers settled into the channel between her shoulder blades. His thumbs swept the smooth skin just below her bra. "Let me touch you."

She might die if he didn't. With his big hands supporting her, she hung on to his strong arms and arched her spine. Her head fell back. Her breath caught as he nudged her sweater over her breasts and lowered his head. Warm breath teased her nipple through the mesh of her bra. Her heart thumped in response, so loud the sound seemed to echo around them.

The noise came again, louder. *Thump. Thump. Thump.* Shane let out a curse, and that's when she realized the noise really *was* echoing around them. Before she could process that realization, he tugged her sweater down and dropped her into her seat. She was still trying to catch her breath when he lowered the fogged driver's side window just enough to reveal Sheriff Kenner standing on the other side, the grip end of his flashlight raised to tap the glass again.

"Is there a problem?" Shane asked, sounding more irritated than contrite.

Kenner took them both in and rolled his eyes. "I'm not going to dignify that with an answer, seeing as how you're both old enough to tell time. Get a room"—his calm, seen-everything stare switched to her—"or a barn. Just get. The park closed at sunset."

"Yes, sir," Shane answered and started the car. Defrost blasting, they buckled their seat belts. Kenner backed up a few steps, waiting in the glare of the Rover's headlights as Shane put the Rover in reverse. He executed one of those quick, efficient three-point turns that took a Y chromosome to pull off and steered the SUV past the THANK YOU FOR VISITING sign.

Thank you for visiting, and don't forget to retrieve your better judgment on the way out. When they hit the main road, she released a breath. "Well, that was fun."

Shane laughed and shot her a knowing look. "You had fun."

His rumpled hair, open shirt, and bad boy grin got the better of her. She felt her lips lifting. "Maybe a little." Which sounded stingy when, in fact, she was a woman who liked her fun. She'd had plenty—with the chef in Manhattan, or the advertising exec in Los Angeles, or the photographer in Charleston—she simply preferred to keep her fun at a safe distance. Recent growth notwithstanding, Magnolia Grove was still a small town at its core. Gossip spread like wildfire, and people weren't shy about stating their opinions. She liked her private life private.

Lucky for her, she was an out-of-sight, out-of-mind kind of girl. Shane had been the one to teach her that lesson, and it had been a killer, coming from him, but since then she'd worked it to her advantage. She enjoyed Manhattan, Los Angeles, and Charleston on her terms, left with a smile on her face, and a *call me next time you're in town* ringing in her ears. She didn't inspire anything deeper from men, and she wasn't looking for it. Casual and long-distance suited her perfectly, because she didn't need Kenner, or Mrs. Pinkerton, or least of all her parents, calling plays from the sidelines of her love life.

"I had fun, too." He kept his eyes on the road but absently reached over and took her hand.

She watched like a bystander as he threaded his fingers through hers and then rested their joined hands on the center console. Hers looked small and delicate cradled in his larger, stronger palm. Holding hands—another one of those pastimes that somehow got left by the wayside in the transition from teenager to adult. The men she had fun with these days weren't expecting to hold her hand. Or go for a drive. Or languish for an evening exploring the agonizing wonderland between all-or-nothing.

His fingers tightened, giving hers a quick squeeze. "The fun doesn't have to be over. There are a thousand detours on this journey. We haven't even gotten close to some of my favorites."

Her hormones bounced and clapped at the thought, but a glance at the glowing numbers on the dashboard clock forced her to tell them to simmer down. "Yeah, it does. My dad's coming over tonight to help me change the furnace filter." Of course, she'd had an ulterior motive when she'd accepted her dad's offer. Having to be home by eight ensured a hard stop on her tour guide duties for the evening, but now she grappled with a troubling mix of want and disappointment she hadn't counted on. Jesus, her head was a mess.

"I know how to change a filter."

"And how would having you do that help my dad escape the house while my mom hosts the monthly meeting of the Magnolia Grove Historic Society?"

"Ah. I see your point." Surprisingly, he didn't disentangle their hands. "Next time."

Now would be the opportunity to restore some order to her messy head, and a woman who knew what was good for her would take it. She cleared her throat. "Um. About next time…"

"Watch what you say. You made a deal, baby girl."

"Don't 'baby girl,' me. I agreed to show you around, not—"

"And you have. I'm trying to get reacquainted with the town, as well as gathering knowledge I need to do my job. That was always the plan."

"This town isn't the only thing you're trying to get

reacquainted with."

He squeezed her hand again. "No, it's not, but you knew that going in. You assumed you wouldn't have any trouble managing my interest, but you didn't count on having interests of your own. Granted, there's more here than either of us bargained for, but the Sinclair I know was never a coward."

Okay. That irked. Maybe she wasn't a free-spirited teenager willing to blindly follow her heart wherever it led, but that didn't make her a coward. It made her mature. Responsible. Grown-up.

"Before you throw the word coward around, ask yourself which one of us left—"

"Shit," he said under his breath as they passed the Whitehall Plantation, following the curve of the road that eventually led to the turn for her driveway. He withdrew his hand from hers to hold onto the wheel as he turned to look at the gracious antebellum structure set back from the road, surrounded by walking oaks.

The furrow in his brow suggested he'd moved on from the topic of her alleged cowardice. "What?"

He faced front again, eyes narrowed, as if solving an equation in his head. "If they fortify the creek banks up here, overflow once handled by the flood fringe will be funneled downstream."

She was no expert, but it seemed logical to her. "I guess so. But there's nothing much downstream. The Pinkerton Family Trust owns the land, and Mrs. Pinkerton wants the natural beauty preserved. Whenever developers come sniffing around—including those in her own family—she throws down the veto. Thanks to her, it's pretty much all woodland, except…"

Her words trailed off as he took the turn to her house. He finished for her. "Except your barn."

Small seeds of concern took root in her stomach. "It's

barely a creek down here. A four-year-old could wade through it half the time. I'm not worried."

He shook his head. "That's not the standard we use. Statistically, the area is part of a hundred-year floodplain. Our engineers calculate the displacement and look at the impact of all that water coming downstream."

The SUV bounced to a halt in front of her barn, and she saw him give the strip of land to the left of her driveway a measuring look — a strip carved over God knew how many years, by the creek that still meandered there, rippling between the bases of tall pines and the branchy trunks of river birch. After a moment, he went on. "I don't need the engineers to tell me that little bank isn't enough to hold back a concentrated influx of water from upstream."

The roots of concern in her gut dug deeper. "Well, what's the solution?"

"The Pinkertons own this land?"

She nodded. "Yes. I own the barn, but it sits on a land lease. Like, a ninety-nine-year land lease. For all intents and purposes, it's mine."

"No, you own the right to peaceful enjoyment of the land, which they won't be able to deliver if the golf course goes in. They'll have to buy you out, and you can use the money to purchase another property." He lifted his phone from the console and began tapping out a note to himself.

"I don't want another property." The concern twisted into anger. "I want *this* property — my barn. It's not model two of phase three of the latest development, interchangeable with half the houses on the market right now. It's special. I can't turn around and find the exact same thing a mile down the road." She turned in her seat, muscles tensing as if ready for battle. "The resort will have to extend the fortification down past my property, or the city can put in drains, or something."

Without looking up from his phone, he said, "There's not

enough frontage to build up the bank, and a new drainage system isn't economically feasible. I don't see anybody giving that option serious consideration when there's only one property at stake."

She stared at him, dumbfounded, for a full minute. He sat there, so rational and unperturbed, oblivious to how he'd just upended her world. "Well, then, they can't have their golf course. This is my *home*, dammit. Maybe you can't understand the concept, since you seem to prefer living out of a suitcase, but I've invested my time, money, and my heart in that place — every board and stone — and I'm not walking away because somebody decides it's the most economically feasible course of action. My home isn't about economics."

He put down his phone and turned to face her. "That's not up to me, Sinclair." His voice remained maddeningly even, but she detected a degree of frustration in the set of his shoulders. "My job is to identify the risks and offer solutions. The city decides which applications to approve or deny. What I *can* tell you is the simplest option usually wins the day."

"Not this time." She shoved the door open and scrambled down. "I'm not accepting a buyout, and Ricky Pinkerton is about to be advised of that fact in no uncertain terms."

Chapter Six

Some things never changed. City hall still inhabited the white-brick colonial next to the Presbyterian Church, the American flag still waved from the flagpole in the town square, and Ricky Pinkerton was still an entitled shithead.

Shane stood on the steps of city hall, between Ricky and Mayor Campbell, listening to Ricky offer up a one-sided, utterly uninformed version of the situation with Sinclair's barn.

"She called me last night in a snit—you know how she is when she's got a bug up her ass—spouting nonsense about the golf course, and hundred-year floods, and how a contract was a contract, and she wasn't selling out. When I told her I didn't know what the fuck she was talking about, she told me this guy"—he jerked a thumb in Shane's direction—"advised her us putting in the golf course turned her barn into an ark. Now, I was able to calm her down, because we go way back, and she respects me, but we don't need some outsider creating problems where those of us who've lived here all our lives know damn well none exist."

"Outsider? Since when am I an outsider? I was born here. We went to high school together, and you've got the bump in your nose to prove it."

He wanted to take the last bit back as soon as he uttered it. Reminding people he used to have a habit of solving problems with his fists undermined his ability to do his job effectively, and antagonizing Ricky wouldn't make the shithead less of a shithead.

Ricky's jaw jutted. "You've been gone for the last ten years. Those of us who stuck around and have family ties here dating back over a century know the Tomochichi Creek never floods." He folded his arms across the chest of his dark-green Calloway sweater and rocked back on his heels. "Never has. Never will."

Shane battled the urge to belt him, right in his professionally re-sculpted nose, but Mayor Campbell beat him to the punch, metaphorically.

"Forgive me, Ricky, but last time I checked, you weren't qualified to give a scientific assessment about the impact of development on a watershed." He turned to Shane. "Do we have any science backing this up?"

"We will. Haggerty's got people with the proper letters after their names at its disposal, but it will take a few weeks to get a report. That said, I know what I'm talking about."

Campbell held up a hand. "I'm not saying you don't, but before we take up the planning commission's time, or put the development's pending permit in doubt, I want to make sure we have our ducks in a row. They've purchased that land and broken ground on the permitted improvements based on the assurances from the city that we support the project. If we need to go back to them now and tell them they've got an environmental issue with the golf course, we'd better be able to support the claim and offer some kind of solution."

"Damn straight," Ricky started in, but Shane shot him a

look that shut him up.

"The way I understand it, Mayor, the investors opted to hold off on submitting the application for the golf course permit until now because they couldn't agree on the final course design." He sent Ricky another hard look. "So, this is a risk they assumed. They rolled the dice."

"They did," Campbell agreed, "but this is the kind of situation where the politician in me has to speak up. This is an important project for Magnolia Grove. The resort revitalizes an historic landmark. It brings jobs and tourist dollars to our economy. I don't do anybody any favors if I put this in front of the planning commission without proper substantiation."

Fair enough. More fair than he might have expected, considering Ricky wasn't the only one on the city council with a horse in this race. Campbell owned and operated the largest construction company in the area, which also happened to be the company doing the work on the resort. An additional permit meant additional work for Campbell Construction. But personal interest or not, the mayor wanted to do things right.

Shane assured Campbell he was on it and headed to his car, already digging his phone out of his pocket. Intellectually, he knew the mayor spoke the truth, but on a personal front, he couldn't quite get over the look on Sinclair's face when he'd told her she'd have to take a buyout. He'd weighed the matter from a strictly logical standpoint, and ignored her emotional attachment to the building. Bottom line? He'd botched the conversation. In his defense, he wasn't used to factoring any personal concerns into his work. This was a first. Well, a second. But the first time his personal concerns had impacted his job, he'd been eighteen and the U.S. Marine Corps had settled the matter for him. He wanted to do better this time. He owed it to both of them.

Once in the car, he called Haggerty and explained the

situation. His boss approached the matter with his usual flair for practicality.

"We can get a civil engineer to do the math and write it up, and I can light a fire under him to expedite the report, but someone's got to manage the brewing conflict in the meantime."

"I'll manage it." Why was Haggerty even bringing it up? Every job involved some amount of bullshit—competing agendas, ambitions, politics—and he had experience dealing with all of it, regardless of whether they were working with a corporate client, a municipality, or a blend of both.

"Normally, there wouldn't be a question in my mind. You have direct, personal familiarity with Magnolia Grove, which makes you the instinctive choice for this assignment, but I don't want that history to cloud your vision."

"My vision is 20/20." He forced himself to loosen his grip on his phone.

"Then I trust you see that this Pinkerton guy is one of the major stakeholders. He's an investor in the resort, and a member of the city council—"

"He's a self-serving asshole. Always has been—"

"And there it is. You've got a personality conflict. So, yeah, I'm concerned. What are you *not* telling me about this self-serving asshole?"

Shane considered glossing over his past with Ricky, but decided against it. Haggerty had a knack for accessing information. If he didn't get a reply from Shane that satisfied him, he'd get the details from another source. "It's nothing. You should be thanking Ricky, actually, because were it not for him, I probably wouldn't be working for you today."

"And to what do I owe his career influence?"

"I broke his nose our senior year of high school. At the prom, to be exact."

"Because?"

"Because I punched him in the face…for not respecting the word 'no' despite his date having said it more than once," he added in response to Haggerty's unspoken question.

"Let me guess. He said, 'God*damn*, Shane, that's a hell of a punch. You should join the Marines'?"

"More like his parents lost their shit and threatened to press charges. Sheriff Kenner suggested I'd be better off taking orders from a commanding officer than a corrections officer. I enlisted in the Marines, which satisfied the Pinkertons that I wouldn't be around to pound the crap out of their son anymore, and I headed off to boot camp right after graduation. The rest, as they say, is history."

"I don't like it. History has a way of repeating itself, and you're already at odds with this guy. Meanwhile, the client in Seattle would happily move their project up if you're available. My gut tells me to pull you off this job and make them happy."

No fucking way. The strength of his reaction surprised him, and it wasn't just a matter of professional pride because he'd never failed to complete an assignment. It went deeper. He didn't *want* to leave yet. He wanted to see this project through with his hometown, but moreover, he wanted to see things through with Sinclair. See where they went. If he left now, the answer would be nowhere. "Seattle can wait. I've got this job under control, and I can handle Pinkerton. This is why you pay me the big bucks."

The other side of the line remained silent for so long, Shane started to scramble for more arguments, but Haggerty finally replied.

"See that you do, son, because from where I'm sitting, that guy looks like a dildo strapped to a boomerang. Don't let him come back and fuck you."

• • •

"Your father said you seemed distracted last night."

Sinclair looked up from her sketch of a necklace a repeat customer had commissioned as a push present for his wife and glanced over to where her cell phone sat on the edge of her drafting table. Her mother's voice filtered from the speaker, thin on maternal concern, despite the observation. She sounded like a seasoned prosecutor lulling a witness into letting her guard down. Sinclair stretched, working the kinks out of her back. She wasn't so easily lulled. "It's nothing. I got into it with Ricky Pinkerton about the proposed golf course for the resort and how it impacts my property."

"So I hear. What a shame if you had to give up that dank, drafty barn."

She bit back a laugh and tipped her face up to enjoy the warmth of the sunlight spilling in from the skylight high above. Her mother made no secret of her disdain for Sinclair's housing choice. Mom wanted her closer—ideally in one of those nice, modern townhomes in the new development about five minutes away from their front door. Cheryl Smith prided herself on knowing what was going on with her girls, and now that Savannah was married and living in Atlanta, the spotlight of all her spare attention had nowhere to land except on her youngest daughter. Sinclair planned to evade that spotlight. "It's not dank or drafty anymore. Dad changed the furnace filter and checked the vent system. I'm toasty."

"Hmm. Maybe you're warm on account of something besides a functioning furnace?"

Huh? "Um. I'm afraid I don't know what you're talking about." But, in actuality, she was afraid she did. The Magnolia Grove grapevine was about to twist around her, and the more she tried to evade, the more likely she'd end up strangled by the damn thing. She hunched in her high, swiveling stool and braced for the inevitable.

"Really? I ran into Sheriff Kenner this morning at the

grocery store."

Shit. Resting her forearms on the drafting table, she leaned forward and hung her head in defeat. "Mom. I'm a grown woman. I'm not going to—"

"Apparently not so grown-up, seeing as how you haven't outgrown having sex in a car at Tomochichi Lookout."

"Jeez, Mom. I wasn't having sex. I was just…" There was no good way to finish the sentence. "…talking."

"Right. You talked so long the sun went down, and the windows steamed up, and one of you had to take off his shirt."

Thank you, Sheriff Kenner. "Crap. Look at the time. I've got to go, Mom."

"Nice try. You're on a cell phone. Go wherever you need to go, I'll just tag along. Now, back to the topic at hand. Shane Maguire. The same boy you danced with at the wedding. I didn't realize you knew him so well."

"I don't." She immediately winced. She didn't want her mom to think she hooked up in cars with strangers. "I mean, not anymore. I know him from high school."

"In that case, we ought to extend our hospitality to your old friend. Invite him to dinner Sunday evening."

She winced again. Mom didn't miss a beat. Her parents hosted dinner every Sunday, but she didn't, as a rule, bring a guest. Definitely not a male guest, and she wasn't going to start now, with Shane. For ten years, she'd managed to keep her parents in the dark about who had been 50 percent responsible for their unscheduled trip to Amsterdam the summer between her sophomore and junior year. Likewise, Shane didn't have a clue about the mess he'd left her to clean up on her own. She planned to keep it that way. "Mom, he's here for work. He's got meetings with the city council, the resort developers, county emergency services, and whatnot. I'm sure he's too busy to come to dinner."

"But he's not too busy to take a drive to the Lookout?"

"I don't even know if I'll see him before Sunday. I don't know his schedule." Absolutely true. He hadn't specified a day for their next tour, and after the way she'd killed the messenger last night when he'd given her the heads-up about the water flow situation, he might not plan to. Cold, hollow disappointment dug into her chest at the thought. She pushed past the ache and concentrated on the annoying needles of guilt prickling the back of her neck. She owed him an apology…

"Well, invite him if you speak to him."

…an apology that would not, under any circumstances, be delivered over Sunday dinner with her parents. Not if she had anything to say about it.

Chapter Seven

"Sinclair, honey, will you get that?"

Shane heard the politely disguised order over the fading chime of the doorbell. Seconds later footsteps echoed on hardwood as someone—presumably Sinclair—approached the front door. He shifted the bottle of wine he held to his left hand, kept the newspaper-wrapped bouquet of sunflowers in his right, and belatedly wondered if she knew her mother had invited him to dinner.

The gleaming, black-painted door swung open. Sinclair stood framed in the entryway, wearing a dark gray sweater dress that hugged her curves, a heart-shaped silver locket on a long chain, and a look of curiosity. The curiosity faded into blank-faced shock as she took him in, and then transformed into an expression he couldn't readily identify, but looked a lot like horror.

Nope. She hadn't known.

Obviously, Cheryl Smith appreciated the value of an ambush, and though she'd made him an unsuspecting accomplice, he had to respect the execution. He leaned against the doorjamb and held out the flowers.

Her glance drifted down to the cheerful yellow blossoms and then flicked back to him. "What is this?"

"They're called flowers, Sinclair. Southern etiquette mandates bringing a gift for the hostess, and Miss Nettie at the flower market told me these are your mother's favorite."

Her eyes narrowed. Instead of gesturing him in, she stepped onto the front porch. "What are you doing here?"

"Your mother invited me to dinner," he replied, using the same hushed tone she'd given him. Then he held up the bottle in his other hand. "I also brought wine. You look like you could use some."

"Sinclair!" Mrs. Smith materialized behind her daughter, her pretty blue eyes sharp, and her smile even sharper. "You may live in a barn, but you weren't raised in one. Invite our guest in."

"You should have brought a bigger bottle," Sinclair muttered under her breath then fixed a smile on her face and stepped back. "Sorry, Mother. I didn't realize you'd invited guests."

"Just Shane. It was all very spur-of-the-moment. I happened to be at city hall on Friday afternoon, and—"

"You *happened* to be at city hall?" Sinclair's eyes narrowed on her mother this time. "Since when do you frequent city hall?"

"It's a lovely building. I had an urge to stop in and appreciate the architecture."

Yeah, she'd been lying in wait. He'd recognized as much the moment he'd stepped out of his office to find her at his door, proclaiming, 'Why Shane Maguire, what a surprise to find you here,' while wearing an expression conveying absolutely no surprise. Meanwhile, *he'd* been disconcerted to realize she'd sought him out, and within seconds, she'd very tidily hemmed him into the dinner commitment. He also recognized a command performance when he received one. The invitation was Mrs. Smith's way of saying, *You've been running around town with my daughter. Her father and I want a look at you.*

Fine by him. They weren't in high school anymore, and he was too old to be sneaking around behind anyone's back. And, ultimately, he didn't want to. He'd kept their relationship secret to be with the girl, because otherwise, it wouldn't have happened, but now he wanted to get to know the woman, and he didn't intend to slink around in shadows to do it.

That said, he wasn't sure exactly what to expect from tonight. He was a little thin on dinner-with-the-parents experience. Deliver aid packages to refugees while under fire from insurgents? No problem. Set up operations on the unstable rubble of earthquake-ravaged settlements to spearhead rescue efforts? Piece of cake. Spend the evening under a parental inquisition? The idea made him sweat.

Back in the day, he never would have been allowed to mow their lawn, much less walk right through the door and sit down to dinner. In his mind, the Smiths represented a "real" family. They lived in an honest-to-God house, ate meals together around an actual table, and her parents stayed reasonably plugged in to what their daughters were up to— and gave a crap for reasons other than how big of a headache the activities might cause them. Given all that, he had to anticipate a grilling this evening, but he figured the flowers might sway things his way. Show Mrs. Smith he'd learned some manners over the last ten years. He held them out.

"These are for you. Rumor has it you're partial to them."

She leaned in to take the flowers. "I am. Thank you, Shane. They're beautiful—"

"Here," Sinclair reached for the bouquet. "I'll put them in water."

"Nonsense." Cheryl intercepted, and he transferred the sunflowers to her. "I'll take care of it." She took the wine as well. "I need to check on dinner, anyway. Please show Shane into the living room and get your father to pour him a drink."

For a moment, Sinclair looked like she wanted to argue, but apparently, she weighed the option of leaving him alone with her father against chaperoning him to the living room and came out on the side of playing chaperone. "This way," she said and walked across the entryway. He followed, appreciating the sway of her hips beneath the clingy gray knit. She led him into a formal living room decorated in shades of blue and white. The sheer abundance of fabric—curtains, sofa, loveseat, wing chairs, and coordinated pillows gracing every cushion—announced a woman had dominated the decorating decisions in the room, but it fit the traditional style of the house.

A tall, dark-haired man unfolded himself from one of the wing chairs when they entered. Bill Smith. Shane wagered Sinclair got her tendency to speak her mind, and her stubborn streak, from her mother, but in terms of coloring and build, she was her father's daughter. Same long, lean frame. Same jet-black hair and dark-blue eyes. Those eyes were calmly sizing him up, which he took as a good sign. The man had reserved his opinion until he could judge for himself.

"Dad, this is—"

"Shane Maguire," her father finished for her, and extended his hand. "Cheryl mentioned something about a guest," he said vaguely at Sinclair's *what-the-hell* look.

"Yes, sir," Shane confirmed and shook his hand.

"Call me Bill, please." He gestured at the lowball glass in his other hand. "Can I get you a drink?"

"Whatever you're having…"

"Bourbon?"

Shane inclined his head. "That works."

"I'll have the same," Sinclair added. "Straight up."

"Two bourbons," Bill repeated and moved to a cabinet containing the bar.

A wall covered in framed photographs caught Shane's eye. He wandered closer. The montage included some family shots, but mostly pictures of Sinclair and Savannah in various stages of growing up. His attention homed in on one featuring a chubby toddler—maybe two years old—wearing a diaper, and an assload of jewelry. Strings of pearls draped her neck. Bracelets of all sizes and styles stacked their way up her little arms. Multiple rings graced every finger. A tiara of necklaces crowned soft, dark curls. The oversize smile on her face pulled a laugh out of him. "I like this outfit."

Sinclair groaned. "Dad, make mine a double."

Her father strolled over, chuckling, and handed Shane a drink. "Pace yourself, kiddo," he said as he handed Sinclair hers. "Your mom's got memory boxes, and she's not afraid to haul them out."

"Jesus, save me." Sinclair took a gulp of the bourbon.

"Dinner's ready," Cheryl called from the archway.

He stepped aside and let her lead them into the dining room. It looked like something out of a Norman Rockwell painting. A crystal chandelier cast a gleam on an oval dining table adorned with matching china, real cloth napkins, and something even rarer in his experience—a home-cooked meal.

Cheryl directed him to a place at the end of the table. Sinclair took what he presumed was her regular spot in the chair to his right. Her father took the seat to his left, and Cheryl settled herself in the chair at the head of the table. She looked innocuous enough, with her tidy blond hair and half smile, but something in that smile told him the game was on, and he was about to square off with a master strategist. She sure as hell had an agenda for this evening, and he was on it.

He didn't have to wait long for her first move. She handed Sinclair a serving bowl full of bacon-laced green beans and leveled her baby blues on him. "So, Shane, how are you enjoying being back in your hometown?"

He helped himself to a piece of fried chicken from the platter Bill held out. "It's interesting," he answered honestly. "Magnolia Grove has grown a lot over the last ten years, but it's held on to its history. Not every community can say the same."

"We're proud of our preservation efforts, which you're now a part of, right?" She gestured toward him. "You're going to help us put the necessary plans in place to ensure we're prepared for any emergency."

He nodded, and accepted a basket of oven-warm rolls from Sinclair. "Create new plans, in some cases, but also coordinate existing plans into a cohesive response."

"An important job. Big responsibility." She tipped her head to the side and considered him. "What brought you to such a career?"

"Uncle Sam."

"That's right," Bill interjected, a forkful of mashed potatoes halted on the journey from plate to mouth. "You joined the service after you graduated, correct? After some dustup with Ricky Pinkerton?"

"Yeah." He rested his fork on his plate and owned up to this part of his past. "I needed an exit strategy. My parents were moving to Illinois, and I wasn't much interested in going. College wasn't in the cards. I hadn't given school much attention up 'til then, and I didn't have the grades or the money. After the altercation with Ricky, his parents wanted me gone, and I liked the sound of the USMC better than I liked my odds of convincing a judge not to send me to county for assault and battery."

"The way I heard it," Cheryl shifted her attention to her daughter, "you were acting in the defense of another. Ricky was liquored up, and had forgotten how to behave like a gentleman."

"That's exactly how it was," Sinclair insisted and then shot him a look. "But as much as I appreciated you riding to my rescue, I didn't need help. I could deal with Ricky—"

"Well, now you can," her father said, and then pointed to Shane with his fork. "After I heard about the incident, I made sure both my girls knew how to *discourage* an overeager suitor."

Was that some kind of a warning? No need. His balls retreated just thinking about the afternoon at the high school when she'd threatened to relocate them to his throat. "I've had a demonstration. Sinclair learned the lesson just fine."

She swatted his arm. "I never unleashed on you, but keep talking, and that will change."

Her father simply sat back in his chair and grinned. "See Cheryl? My work here is done."

Cheryl rolled her eyes and then leveled them on Shane again. "How did the Marines transition into your position at Haggerty?"

Sinclair stilled, and he sensed her interest from a foot away. He would have shared the information at any time, but, for whatever reason, she'd refrained from asking.

"After boot camp, I was selected for a newly created MOS—a special unit formed to spearhead domestic and international crisis response and relief missions. I spent four years hopping from one disaster to the next, assessing needs, establishing security, and coordinating responses. Then my commanding officer, Jack Haggerty, founded Haggerty Emergency Management. When my tour ended, he made me an offer I couldn't refuse. I joined his firm. With his encouragement, I filled out my skillset with a degree and certificate in emergency management. Now I'm the VP for disaster planning and crisis management."

"Impressive," Bill said and nodded.

He shrugged. "I fell into it, for the most part. Early in boot camp I hit a snag—or created one for myself, depending on whom you ask. Jack helped unsnag me. He sat me down and told me he thought I displayed stronger-than-average protective instincts, which he wanted, and piss-poor impulse control, which concerned him, to put it mildly. But he gambled on being able to cultivate the instincts and instill some discipline. The gamble paid off, for me."

"And now Magnolia Grove reaps the benefit of your expertise," Cheryl noted. "You get to reconnect with your hometown. Your"—she gestured to Sinclair—"friends."

"Mom…" Sinclair's voice vibrated with warning.

Cheryl ignored her daughter, and looked Shane squarely in the eyes. "Now that you're back, will you be staying?"

• • •

Sinclair battled the urge to bang her head against the table. Her mother didn't always bother with subtlety, but even the thickest blockhead couldn't help but pick up on the underlying question in this latest inquiry. Namely, *What are your intentions regarding our daughter?*

Shane was no blockhead. She turned to her father and pointed at her mother. "Can't you get a leash on this?"

"I'm definitely considering the option," Shane replied, as if she hadn't spoken. "Sinclair's been showing me around, and I can't deny Magnolia Grove has a certain appeal."

"That's very nice of you, honey," Cheryl said to her daughter.

Ha. Nice was not the word. "Well, when he came to me with the request, I really couldn't say no."

"Of course not," Cheryl agreed. "The least you could do is help an old friend rediscover his home. Although"—she paused and sent her daughter a mild gaze Sinclair knew better than to take at face value—"I wasn't aware you two knew each other well growing up."

"We didn't." Sinclair said the words fast, but not quite fast enough to cut off Shane's reply.

"We got to know each other toward the end of my senior year," he said, and offered her a slow smile. "After I broke Ricky's nose, a whole lot of people wanted my hide, but she stuck up for me." He covered her hand where it rested on the table, and squeezed.

She kept hers absolutely still, in a silent plea for him to stop talking, but he didn't read her mind.

"She tried to tell everyone what actually happened, and, for what it's worth, I think Kenner believed her. But Ricky had all his friends telling a different story, and Kenner knew I didn't stand a chance if his parents pressed charges, so he did his best to resolve the situation in a way that didn't leave a mark on my permanent record."

"It was nothing," she said, trying to end the conversation.

Her mother's brow furrowed, and she turned to Sinclair. "So, you two got to be friends before the summer you—?"

"We were *not* friends." The sharpness of her words drew everyone's eyes to her. She took a deep breath and told herself to reel it in. "Friends isn't the right word. We just...we hung out a few times..." Shit.

Shane turned her hand over and wove their fingers together, seemingly oblivious to how cold and stiff hers were. "I don't agree," he said in a low voice. "We may not have spent much time together before I left, but I considered you my best friend."

The moment took on its own momentum, spinning her around, pulling her down like a boat caught in a whirlpool. From a place beyond rescue, she watched her mother's mouth drop open to release a small, almost imperceptible gasp. Eyes filled with new awareness darted to Shane and then shot a silent question at Sinclair.

Get this contained. Now. She leapt out of her chair, and grabbed her plate. "I'll help you clear, Mom." Brilliant.

Her mother nodded and then stood as well, picking up her own plate and the basket of rolls. "Thank you, dear."

Sinclair stacked Shane's plate on hers, turned, and practically ran through the small butler's pantry to the kitchen.

Her mom came in, hot on her heels, and put her dishes on the white-and-black marbled counter by the deep farmhouse sink. With a regal air Sinclair could never hope to emulate, she turned and regarded her daughter. "He's the one."

It wasn't a question, so she didn't offer up an answer. She put her dishes on the counter with shaking hands and retreated to the opposite side of the kitchen, until the island backstopped her.

Her mother shook her head. "Sinclair, for heaven's sake, if you were seeing him that spring, why didn't you bring him around and introduce us? You obviously had strong feelings for him, and it seems he returned them."

"You and Dad wouldn't have approved. You would have put a stop to it."

"That's not true."

"Really? His brother was in jail, he'd just gotten in trouble for punching Ricky, and he was leaving for boot camp at the start of summer. What part of that would you have liked?"

"The part where I knew what was going on with my daughter," she retorted, color rising in her cheeks. "I would have liked the chance to talk to you about the decisions you were making, and…" She broke off and smoothed a hand over her curls, taming them as she tamed her temper. As a rule, her mom didn't choose to belabor things that couldn't be changed.

Sinclair couldn't agree more. "Don't tell Dad. Please."

Her mother dropped her hand to her hip. "What your father knows or doesn't know isn't an issue anymore. You're an adult, not a teenager he feels like he failed to protect. The issue is whether Shane knows he almost—"

"Shhh!" She cast a glance toward the door. "Keep your voice down."

Pursed lips and crossed arms greeted her request. "He doesn't know. Oh, Sinclair…"

"Sinclair *what*? It happened a long time ago." Restless energy propelled her. She paced the short distance until she stood in front of her mother. "It's over. Nothing came of it."

"Not nothing." The calm evaporated. "Don't you *dare* tell me about nothings. Your father and I rushed to a hospital a continent away, in a dead panic."

"I'm sorry." Guilt swamped her, again, as an image of her pale-faced parents flanking her bedside swam into her mind.

"Goddammit." Her mother rarely cursed. A rarer thing, still, for her to rub her eyes and let her shoulders slump. She blew out a breath and looked up. "I'm not trying to make you sorry. I'm trying to make you see it wasn't nothing." She made air quotes around the word. "It impacted you, and you've born the burden on your own."

Surprise had her straightening her spine. Did her family see her as some kind of broken wing? She wasn't. "I'm perfectly fine."

"You keep a part of yourself closed off. It's like you have a perimeter and nobody's allowed too close."

"Mom…"

"The barn? That's isolationism, right there. And the men. Oh, yes," she went on, when Sinclair opened her mouth to disclaim them. "I know there are men in your life, but you keep them far away."

Heat crept into her face. "There's been no reason to bring any of them around. They're not…important." Jesus. What an awful thing to admit to a parent. Feeling dirty, she automatically took a step back.

"Honey…" Her mom took hold of her shoulders to keep her in place. "You don't give anyone a chance to be important." Then, in her mother's trademark way of cutting to the heart of the matter, she asked, "Did you love him?"

A lump lodged in her throat. Oversize and jagged. She actually had to swallow hard to get past it. "Mom, I was a kid. It was ten years ago…"

"Fine. It was the past, but it's his past, too. What happened involved him, and he ought to know—"

Panic kicked in, cold, desperate, and not in a listening mood. "No, it happened to me. It's *my* past. Mine. And I shouldn't have to share it if I don't want to—"

The sound of a throat clearing cut her off. She looked up to find Shane filling the kitchen entryway, a carefully neutral expression on his face and plates balanced in his hands. "Sorry to interrupt."

One question filtered through her mind—*How much did he hear?*—before her brain cells locked up. Luckily, her mother suffered no such affliction. She swept forward. "No apology necessary." With the deftness of a born hostess, she took the plates from him and flashed him a charming smile. "We were rudely sidetracked. We don't usually make our guests clear the table."

He offered up his own, equally effective version of a charming smile. "Sorry, ma'am. You can take the man out of the Marines, but you can't take the Marines out of the man. I clean up after myself. And, unfortunately, I have to go. I have a client in Australia who discovered a data breach, and I need to jump on a call in thirty minutes."

Her mom transferred the dishes to the counter and wiped her hands on a lemon-yellow towel. "Oh, mercy. That's a shame. Sinclair, the key lime pie is in the fridge. Fix him up a slice to take with him."

It took her a moment to process the instructions, but then she jumped to do her mother's bidding as all the information filled in the bigger picture. The sooner she got his slice of pie in a Tupperware box, the sooner he'd be gone and this nerve-wracking minefield of an evening would be over.

"Here," she practically shoved the plastic container at him. "See you later."

"Sinclair, see our guest to the door, please." Her mother used the same tone she'd used when telling a five-year-old Sinclair things like, *Give your Aunt Penelope a kiss.* Aunt Penny had been two hundred years old and smelled like mothballs. Shane, on the other hand…

"Yeah, Sinclair. Walk me to the door." His lips lifted into a grin, but his eyes didn't join the festivities. They assessed her with something that looked a lot like concern.

Like the diminutive bulldozer she was, her mother ushered everyone out of the kitchen. They were through the house, exchanging thank-yous and good-byes, and then she was alone on the front porch with Shane.

He set the pie container on the porch rail. "Anything you'd like to tell me?" His eyes found hers.

"Well played, with the conference call. I'll have to remember that one." Sarcasm was her superpower, thankfully, because the last thing she wanted to do on her parents' doorstep was have an honest conversation with him about the past. "Good-night." She turned and reached for the doorknob.

The next thing she knew, she was locked tight against a solid barrier of muscle while a brutally effective tongue swept the sarcasm right out of her mouth. The only things left were raw, and honest, and utterly impossible to deny. The present expanded to blot out past and future. Time condensed into this single instant, and she clung to it, ready to abandon caution and pride for the chance to wallow in want so strong it hurt, need now infused with some new, dangerously addictive promise she couldn't resist, along with a sweet aftertaste of the past. She'd learned the hard way not to put much stock in his promises. When he finally raised his head, she went onto her tiptoes to give chase, sinking her teeth into his lower lip to punish him for…everything. Coming back. Stirring up old memories and new feelings.

A groan—more pain than pleasure—rumbled from deep in his chest, but he cupped her cheeks and used his thumbs to wipe away tears she hadn't realized had gathered at the corners of her eyes. Appalled, she drew back, only to be brought up short by his arms. Her defense mechanisms took control of her vocal cords.

"Go away."

He could have interpreted the rude instruction to apply just to the here and now, and the fact that he had a call to attend to, but the set of his jaw and the determined look in his eyes told he knew damn well what she'd meant. He kissed her again, brushing his lips over hers. "No."

Oh, but he would. Eventually. She sniffed inelegantly and shoved the heel of her hand against his immovable shoulder. "If you knew what was good for you, you'd get in that fancy rental of yours and drive straight out of town."

"Uh-uh. I only just got here." His lips skimmed her eyelid with heart-stopping gentleness. "You still owe me four tours. Next one is tomorrow morning. Be ready at nine."

He stepped away without waiting for her reply and made his way down the front walkway.

"Shane—"

"Tell you mother thanks for dinner," he called from the street. The slam of his car door punctuated the comment.

Suddenly exhausted, she leaned against the porch rail and watched him pull away from the curb. When his taillights disappeared from view, she scrubbed her hands under her eyes and inhaled the cool night air. Oh, yeah. She'd be thanking her mother, all right.

Chapter Eight

Shane made a right turn onto Sawmill Road and glanced at his rearview mirror to ensure the Tahoe behind him followed.

Annoyance simmered under his skin. He'd lost the car battle again. Sinclair had met him at her door this morning and announced she'd drive herself because she planned to run errands after their tour. More like she planned to keep him at a distance.

He planned to keep her guessing. When she'd asked where they were going, he'd simply told her to follow him into town and park at the public lot the city had installed a few years ago to accommodate visitors and employees of the shops and businesses downtown. Disclosing their destination would have been the mature thing to do, but after a shitty night spent stewing over the scene he'd stumbled into yesterday evening in the Smiths' kitchen, he'd bypassed mature. She was keeping a secret from him, and he was just petty enough to give her a taste of her own medicine.

Seeing Sinclair and her mother standing close, arguing in rapid whispers, had told him there was an elephant in the room. The caged look on her face when he'd cleared his throat had told him plainly enough the elephant was him.

She didn't want to talk about it. That much was clear. But the defensiveness she'd thrown at him from day one was starting to piss him off. If she had something to say, she could say it to his face. He deserved that much. No, things hadn't gone the way they'd planned ten years ago, and yes, he'd fumbled the ball. But she'd ended the game. That call had been all hers. No discussion. No dialogue of any kind. She'd imposed the forfeit with a wall of silence he'd been in no position to break through—then. The USMC had owned his ass, and they hadn't been inclined to give him time off to go confront the underage girl dodging his calls and sending his letters back unopened.

Consider her the one that got away and move on.

Screw that. Things were different now. He was here, and they were on a level playing field. She could use silence, or sarcasm, or plain old evasion, but none of those tricks would work on him. He was going to shatter her precious wall.

He signaled and slowed to make the turn into public parking. Unwilling to provide her with any clue of their specific destination, he slid into a slot in the dead center of the lot.

She pulled in next to him.

Brace yourself, baby girl, he thought and turned away to gather up his phone, keys, and wallet from the caddy between the front seats. A few seconds later he approached her Tahoe.

She sat still and straight in the driver's seat, her long hair spilling like ink over the shoulders of a snuggly, off-white poncho-type thing, her chin flirting with the folded edge of the turtleneck. She stared out the window, ostensibly taking in the dichotomy of downtown Magnolia Grove, where buildings put up over a century ago served as a backdrop to the ebbing rush hour bustle of laptop-toting commuters fixated on their phone screens. In reality, he sensed she was a million miles away from all of it—the bustle, the buildings. Him.

A little flinch from her as he opened her door announced she'd dialed back into the here and now. "Where are we going?"

The question sounded casual enough, but Sinclair's pale cheeks and the tight press of her lips suggested more than idle curiosity. She hid her eyes behind dark sunglasses, even though the morning clouds crowding the skyline promised rain.

"You'll see." He offered her a hand as she slid out of the car, and kept the light hold on her arm as he steered them toward the west end of the lot and the two-level, brick building with rounded front edges and other deco flourishes proclaiming it a landmark of late 1930s architecture.

She dug in her heels and turned to him, eyebrows so high they showed above the rims of her sunglasses. "The bus depot?"

"A very important entry and exit point in the event of certain emergencies." Also a risky choice, considering the last time they'd been here together, they'd been teenagers, pledging their love to each other and promising no amount of time or distance would tear them apart. Then—big surprise— it had, leaving a sting of regret ten years had never completely erased. Maybe the breakup had been inevitable, given their ages, and everything else, but if he hoped to put the past behind them, they needed to have the conversation she'd been ducking for over a week. Assign blame, if that's what it took. He'd shoulder his share, but he would damn well know exactly what failings she was holding him accountable for, because at this point, he wasn't sure of anything except there was something she wasn't telling him.

Everything he knew with a certainty about them ended here, at this depot, which made it the obvious place to start the what-happened-after discussion. The one that took them places she didn't want to go. He gave her arm a little tug. "Come on."

She fell into step beside him but took her arm back and hid both beneath the folds of her poncho. For warmth? Or to discourage him?

Yeah, sorry. Not that easily discouraged. He moved in close enough her shoulder brushed his arm as they walked. Memories swept in, more sensory than visual. Last time they'd taken this walk together, he'd had her nestled against him, anxious to soak up every touch until the last possible second. She'd rested her head on his shoulder, face pressed against his neck, hands clinging to his waist, relying on him to guide them. Together they'd woven themselves into a private cocoon of exquisite misery.

He hadn't needed to dissuade family from coming down to see him off. His parents had moved the week before. He'd packed his shit, sold his truck, and sofa-surfed with friends until his ship-out date. Her parents had thought she was at the mall in Norcross doing some last-minute shopping for her summer in Europe. Instead, she'd met him behind the Presbyterian Church, and within five seconds of sliding into the shiny little Beetle she'd gotten for sweet sixteen, she'd somehow managed to straddle his lap, and he'd buried himself inside her one last time, rocking together with desperate enthusiasm right there in the shadow of the church. Later, riding on the bus to Parris Island, he'd tasted her on his tongue, smelled her on his skin, and endured a hollow ache of longing so deep it had felt like a hole in his chest.

He held open one side of the double glass doors and ushered her inside the depot. She perched her sunglasses on the top of her head and looked around, blinking as her eyes adjusted to the light. "They've expanded since…" Her voice drifted off.

True. The once bare-bones facility now boasted two ticket windows, an electronic schedule board detailing a dozen arrivals and departures, a waiting area full of interlocked seats, and a concession counter complete with a couple of bistro tables lined up against the window wall facing the lot now designed to accommodate up to three buses at once. They'd hit it during a lull, after the morning rush of local and long-distance commuters but before the next wave of arrivals from regional locations, so only a few people occupied the waiting area.

He headed in the direction of the concession counter. "Coffee?"

"Um. Sure."

"I'll get it. Have a seat."

With a less-than-enthusiastic nod, she headed to one of the tables. He took a moment to enjoy the way faded denim hugged her thighs and disappeared into tan sheepskin boots, and then went to the counter and ordered. The bored guy behind the register tore himself away from his phone long enough to fill Shane's order and promptly resumed crushing candy.

Shane made his way over to the table she'd selected, aware her guarded eyes watched his every step. When he put her coffee in front of her, he said, "Let's talk."

Reading body language sometimes took keen observational skills, but not in this case. She pulled her arms off the table and crossed them. The rubber sole of one boot tapped out a soft, impatient rhythm on the black-and-white tile floor. Interpretation? *Hell no.*

"About what?"

He rested his forearms on the table, and leaned into the space she'd vacated, deliberately pursuing her. Silently telling her he wasn't going to back off this time. "About secrets. Specifically, the one you're keeping from me."

Her chin went up. "You're paranoid."

"You're defensive. You're holding something against me, but I can't fix it if I don't know what it is."

"Maybe I don't appreciate how you glide back into town after a decade and expect me to be waiting—ready and willing to pick up where we left off?"

Not fair. He hadn't *expected* a thing, and she knew it, but he also recognized someone trying to pick a fight to avoid a conversation. He refused to return the verbal body shot and instead focused on the real question buried in hers. "Where *did* we leave off, Sinclair? I remember standing right there"—he pointed out the window—"telling you I loved you and listening to you tell me the same. And then you never responded to my letters or answered my calls—"

"What letters? What calls? You mean the ones that didn't start until *months* after you left?" She leaned in now, too, her icy reserve burned away by a wave of genuine outrage. "You blew me off for the entire summer—longer. By the time you finally decided to give me the time of day, I—"

"You moved on." He lowered his voice. "It's fine, Sinclair. I get it. You could have dropped me a line to let me know as much, but you were only sixteen, and maybe you didn't know how to say it. You don't have any reason to feel guilty or defensive."

She jerked upright as if he'd slapped her. "Fuck *you*, Shane Maguire. I don't feel guilty, or defensive. I'm angry. Because—because—" She literally clamped her mouth shut, turned away, and inhaled a deep breath through her nose.

There was the wall again. This time frustration got the better of him. "Because it took me longer to get in touch than you expected? I was in boot camp, for God's sake, not on a vacation. We talked about this before I left. The Marines owned me during that time. Thirteen weeks of no cell phone, no texting, no computers. Limited opportunity to write, but

I couldn't do that anyway, because you were in Europe all summer. I would maybe…*maybe*…earn a phone call—"

"I had my phone the entire time. It never rang. Not once. There was a point when I would have sold my soul just to hear your voice. I marked off every day of thirteen weeks on my calendar, waiting like some pathetic idiot. But after four months of silence? No. Just…no." Still stubbornly looking away, she brought her coffee to her lips.

The sharp note of betrayal in her voice stirred his guilty conscience. Turns out he had defensive reflexes as well. "Jesus Christ, Sinclair, that was ten fucking years ago. Something I didn't plan happened my first week of boot camp, okay, and it screwed up my timeline. So maybe you could cut me a little slack?"

Coffee exploded from her mouth on a choking cough. She coughed again, into a napkin this time, and then drew in a careful breath. When she lowered the napkin, she looked at him as if she wanted to slug him. "Something unplanned happened to *you*?"

Fuck it. The incident was not his proudest moment, but apparently even after all this time, he needed to justify being out of touch longer than expected. He waited until she stopped mopping coffee from the table and looked at him again. "I got sent to the brig for decking the drill instructor. One of the recruits in my unit fell out during a training run. The guy—Salcido—was down, clutching his knee and insisting he couldn't move, but the DI wouldn't back off. He kept yelling, 'On your feet, recruit.' Salcido kept saying he couldn't. Then the DI kicked him, and I lost it. Next thing I knew I was standing over my DI, with my knuckles on fire, watching his eye swell shut."

"You came to his defense," she said, sounding strangely distant. Her face went blank.

"I came this close to getting bounced"—he held up his

hand, finger and thumb a half inch apart—"but the other recruits in the unit spoke up. Even so, it took three weeks for the Corps to investigate the incident and clear me. They funneled me into the next group of new recruits, and I spent the following twelve weeks on my best fucking behavior, because there is zero margin for error during a second chance."

"I-I can only imagine." Color slashed across her cheekbones, like crimson flags against her otherwise pale skin.

"Now you know the whole story. So, here's the thing, Sinclair—the U.S. Marines saw fit to give me a second chance. Maybe you could do the same?"

. . .

Her heart stuttered in her chest. So stupid, because explanations hardly mattered after all this time. Ultimately, his didn't change a thing. But even so, her world tilted off-center, leaving her scrambling to rebalance her internal compass and get it pointed in a safe direction. That turned out to be the door, and after mumbling a weak-assed, "I'm not doing this," through numb lips, she managed to propel herself toward it, dodging a wave of passengers flooding into the depot from a Greyhound she hadn't even noticed arriving.

Over the din, she heard Shane call her name, but she kept moving, shoving through the double doors and gulping in breaths of burning-cold air as she broke into a run. A car screeched to a halt to avoid plowing into her. Shane called her name again—alarmed this time—but also farther away. She dug her key out of her pocket while she rushed to her car. Thank God for keyless entry and a start-button ignition, because shaking hands would have prevented her from sliding a key into a lock. The battery juiced life into the dashboard displays, but the engine thwarted her for one panicked second. She gunned the gas and got no response, until she finally realized she still had it in park. She shoved the stick to drive, and the Tahoe lurched forward.

A hand slammed down on her hood. She jumped, and looked over in time to watch Shane shout her name once more. Anger dominated his voice now. She jerked the wheel left and shot toward the parking lot exit, bouncing hard as her tire hit the curb on her way out.

Urban off-roading, she thought hysterically and gripped the wheel a little harder. All she could think of was getting away. Getting herself under control before she said something she couldn't unsay about old mistakes she couldn't undo.

Her cell buzzed from the depths of the purse she'd left on her passenger seat. After a moment it stopped, then started again. She ignored the noise but steered at a more cautious speed through downtown. With every mile she put between her and the bus depot, she breathed a little easier—until she got stuck behind a cement truck just outside the Whitehall Plantation and noticed a black Range Rover coming up fast in her rearview mirror.

Adrenaline kicked in again. The kind that took control of her nervous system without any oversight from her brain. She hit the accelerator and pulled into the oncoming lane. A flatbed hauling a backhoe lumbered toward her, chugging up the hill with all its unwieldy momentum. She floored it, zipping past the cement truck and swinging back into her lane before the flatbed driver finished blowing his horn at her.

The sharp turn into her driveway forced her to slow down, but apparently, Shane possessed advanced driving skills, because he took it much faster. The Rover skidded into the turn, took a hard, fishtailing drift to account for physics, and then the big back tires spat gravel as he accelerated out of the maneuver.

Physics might not be her strong suit, but she knew math well enough. How long would it take one mad-as-hell man driving forty miles per hour to overtake one chickenshit woman driving half that speed? More than the twenty feet she had left in her driveway. Running wouldn't work. The situation called for a new strategy. Control the confrontation. Shane was about to meet the stone wall of her resolve.

She pulled the Tahoe to a halt, jumped down from the driver's seat, and slammed the door while the Rover screeched to a halt. The driver's door opened before the vehicle completely stopped moving. That should have given her pause, but she gritted her teeth and set off toward him at a righteous pace…until he got out of the car and she saw his face.

Holy shit. Crashing headfirst into a Peterbilt would have been the easy way out. She barely registered drawing to a stop, possibly taking a step back, as he closed in on her like a dark angel—a dark angel looking deceptively mortal with his disheveled hair, black crewneck sweater, and dark jeans, but the fury coming off him like unearthly energy belied anything casual in his intentions. It electrified the air around him, turning the atmosphere volatile and dangerous.

A stone wall, she reminded herself and lifted her chin. "Get out."

He just kept coming, forcing her to cede ground until the back end of the Tahoe brought her up short. "If you ever do anything that reckless again, I swear to God you won't sit for a week."

Her control faltered, and something snide and impulsive took over. "Oh, honey, when it comes to reckless, you just saw the tip of the iceberg. You should run now, before I really show you the meaning of the word."

He moved closer, until they stood toe-to-toe. "Bring it, baby girl. Take your best shot."

The crack of her palm connecting with his cheek shattered the silence. His head snapped back and to the side. Vibrations shimmered up her arm while red bloomed on his cheek. A stunned part of her reeled at the unpremeditated violence inside her. She wasn't above taking a shot at someone—she'd literally slapped sense into her own brother-in-law just a few months ago—but up until now she'd always known what she intended to do before she did it. This time she'd been a passenger in her body. A detached observer. Slowly, he turned his face back to her, his eyes cool and assessing. "Ten years, and that's the best you can do?"

Detachment burned away so fast she went lightheaded, and control spun far out of reach. She felt her muscles tensing this time. Heard the whoosh of her hand cutting through the air, before another crack echoed around them. Words with a venomous taste coiled on her tongue, so foul and bitter she spat them out. "I hate you."

Big hands cupped her jaw, holding her in place while hard shivers rattled through her. "No, you don't," he murmured and lowered his mouth to hers.

She wanted to pull away. She told herself to pull away. But God damn him, she couldn't. And he knew it. He took his sweet time, moving his lips over hers in unhurried passes, conveying an unmistakable message with every slow assault. *Hit at me all you want. I'm not going anywhere.*

It shook her, that certainty—his absolute confidence, regardless of what she threw at him. Need swept in like a storm front, bigger than her anger and impervious to her boundaries. Her back arched to press their bodies closer, and his arm clamped around her waist to help her do it. "I do," she insisted, knowing full well she was losing this battle. "I hate you…"

The words ended in a moan as he leaned into her, moving his chest over hers and dragging layers of fabric over her tight nipples.

"You hate this?" He reached under her poncho, under

her camisole, and palmed her breasts. His hands were harder and rougher than they'd been in the old days, but it only made her reaction all the more forceful. Something far too intense to call pleasure tore through her, dissolving her muscles and buckling her knees.

He caught her, dragged her into his arms so her legs had no option but to wrap around his waist and her arms had no choice but to twine around his neck. Meanwhile, his mouth consumed whatever answer she might have given before it reached her lips. The trees whirled overhead as he moved, and the next thing she knew, he had her braced against the side of the Rover, one hand supporting her ass, the other busy inflicting an equally staggering caress to her other breast. "I hate it," she managed, over another moan.

"I remember." His ragged exhale fanned her raw lips. "I remember how much you hated this, too."

A sharp cry of surprise jostled out of her when he hitched her up higher, shoved her clothes out of the way, and fastened his mouth on her breast. The contact immediately calmed something needy inside her, comforting an ache nobody over the last ten years had been able to soothe. Sensations, familiar and overwhelming as any long-overdue homecoming, wrung a grateful sigh out of her. She sagged forward, hugging his head, losing herself in the irresistible pull of the moment and the memories. Then his mouth began moving, and memories scattered as heat seared her from the inside out. Before, he'd always touched and kissed her breasts gently at first. Not now. He used lips and tongue and teeth to draw her in, widening his jaw to take…consume…devour.

His lack of restraint stripped her down to an elemental state, beyond flesh, or bone, to a few brutal pulse points—lips, nipples, and the biggest pulse of all, pounding relentlessly between her legs.

She couldn't keep still. Her feet felt clumsy in her boots,

but she dug the soles into his calves, clawed at his back through his sweater, and did the best she could to press every throbbing part of her against him. He must have felt her urgency. Must have. But he wouldn't be rushed. He used that ruthless mouth on her until she couldn't take any more. She gripped his hair and pulled hard enough to force his head up. Then she closed her eyes so she didn't have to face him and slammed her mouth down on his.

After one heady moment allowing her ownership, he took control of the kiss. With a hand at the back of her head, he positioned her just where he wanted her and proceeded to plunge his tongue deep, retreat, and plunge again. Over and over, so her mouth filled with his taste, but it only made her hungry for more. Bigger, deeper, harder…more.

She struggled to work her hand between their bodies, but the way he had her pinned between cold steel and his hot, hard body prevented her from reaching her goal.

He eased back, lowering her by degrees until her toes scraped the gravel. When she was securely on her feet, he took her hand and guided it to the thick ridge straining the front of his jeans. Held it there, absolutely still for one long moment while a ridiculously attractive flush rose in his cheeks. He let out a tortured breath and lowered his forehead to hers. His dark gaze locked on her, he took his hand away and whispered, "How about this, Sinclair? Do you hate this?"

"Uh-huh." Her hands shook as she tugged his fly open. "I hate it…" And then she was holding it, stroking, relearning landmarks the years had subtly altered—the smooth, blunt tip, the sensitive opening that still dragged a groan out of him when she explored it with her thumb, the flare of flesh marking the transition from head to shaft. It wasn't until she'd wrapped her hand around the thickest part, wringing another low sound from his throat, that she realized the pressure in her chest was building to match the pressure at her core. Longing took many forms, and all of them were about to have their way with her. And she wasn't strong enough to stop any of it. Gripping his hips for balance, she dropped to her knees. "I really hate it," she said again, then put her lips against the tip.

His head dropped forward, and his fingers tangled in her hair. "Jesus. Show me. Punish me."

She took him into her mouth, leading with her tongue, stretching her lips to surround him. Taste and scent unleashed vivid, sensory flashbacks…the thrill of discovering every mysterious inch of him, the pride of making him tremble for her, the joy of hearing him say her name over and over again as he lost control. The memories stung her eyes and tightened her chest. Then he groaned and gave a rough, potentially involuntary thrust. The move generated heat, and friction, and raw new needs.

Desperate to satisfy them, she planted her knees, tipped her head to the most accommodating angle, and offered him everything. Just the way she'd learned to do during those long spring nights a lifetime ago.

"Fuck, Sinclair." He gripped her chin and stared down at her. "You have no idea how much I missed you. You couldn't possibly. Leaving you felt like losing a vital organ." Then he thrust again, and again, in rapid succession. She'd braced for fast, and deep. Wanted it. But he remembered a few things, too—like how easily he could reduce her to a quivering mess by holding back, teasing her with quick, shallow strokes. Punishment, she discovered, cut both ways, and could be unbearably sweet as well as heartrendingly painful. Despite his restraining hand, she went deep, gorging herself on all of it—past, present, sweetness, pain…him—knowing full well it was too much, but still would never be enough.

A sob pushed its way into her throat. She choked it back and hoped he attributed the artless noise to her overeager struggle to take as much of him as she possibly could. His big hand stroked her jaw. "Easy, baby girl," he murmured and then sliced her heart open with one careful fingertip, running it over her lips, tracing the seam where their bodies met. How had she forgotten the way he did that? Or how one simple gesture could make her feel so…cherished?

Except he'd taught her she wasn't the kind of girl men cherished, and now he'd come back and undermined the lesson with a single explanation. How dare he? Because in doing so, he also took away her justification for distributing blame for what happened that summer to him, which meant she had to accept it all. "I hate you," she said, reminding him, reminding *herself*, and then lowered her head to finish him. Exorcise him. Claim one harshly honest moment and be done with him.

But a strong arm hooked under her shoulder and hauled her up until her face hovered just millimeters from his. Her lips throbbed from the friction of his cock sliding between them. His taste coated her tongue. Deprivation set in, sudden and painful, but maddeningly patient green eyes stared into hers, taking stock, unquestionably seeing the deprivation, and the need, but looking past them to things she didn't want him to see. Didn't want anyone to see.

"No, you don't. You wish you did, but you don't."

"I do. I—"

His mouth slammed down on hers, cutting her off. The sense of deprivation immediately subsided, replaced by the bite of his teeth and the lash of his tongue. His leg slid between hers. A hand on her ass lifted her onto her toes. Her hands found his shoulders, and she held on as he rocked her against his hard thigh.

Her moan of pleasure couldn't be stifled, nor her body's greedy response. Within moments she was fighting the steady rhythm he'd set, grinding against him like some kind of animal, while their mouths came together, parted, came together again.

"You missed me," he whispered. "Say it."

Jesus, she had. Desperately. "No."

Hands reached between them and tore her jeans open, then long, sure fingers delved into her panties, stroked there long enough to ensure they both knew how wet she was, and then his lips curved into a smile. "Part of you did."

"I hate to break it to you, Shane, but a lot of men can do that for me." She tossed her head back in a patented bitch move. "A lot of men have."

His eyes darkened, but his smile kicked up a notch, to downright cocky. "Nobody can do it for you like me, though."

That was all the warning she got. Her breath burst out in a shocked gasp as he slid two fingers inside her, curling upward to let her know what was coming. The heel of his hand settled against her clit like it had been made to fit there. She writhed. Couldn't stop herself.

"You remember how I first taught you to come, baby girl? Just like this? You'd squirm around, like you're doing, trying like hell to get yourself there. Then I'd reach up inside this tight…little…pussy"—he reached as he spoke, and she rose up onto her tiptoes—"find the magic spot, and you'd come all over my hand. Just for me."

He found it. Unerringly. Her vision blurred, and she came in a rush—as if she'd been waiting for his touch for ten long years.

Chapter Nine

"Still hate me?"

The question taunted her from somewhere beyond the pounding of her pulse in her ears. "Yes," she muttered but doubted he heard her, considering she leaned into him with her face pressed against his sweater and his sturdy frame supporting her. If not for his arm around her and the hand still lingering protectively between her legs, she'd be a puddle at his feet.

A moment to catch her breath—that's all she needed—and maybe another to get her misfiring nervous system under control, and then she'd push off him and barricade herself safely behind the barn doors. The point when she'd have to deal with the fallout from today's little trip down memory lane was closing in fast, and she preferred no witnesses to her personal meltdown.

But apparently, he had heard her reply, and he wasn't done trying to prove her a liar yet. Everything went weightless, and then she landed in the driver's seat of the Rover with her elbows propped on the center console and her legs dangling out the open door. He stepped between her knees, filling the door, blocking everything from her view except him.

"Was that orgasm you're still shaking from an example of how badly you hate me? Three more minutes, Sinclair, and you're going to despise me."

She scrambled for handholds on the seat and steering wheel as he tugged her jeans and panties down past her hips. Another tug left them bunched around the tops of her boots.

"Remember the second way I taught you to come?"

Oh, sweet Jesus. She did. But he didn't give her a chance to answer. He hitched her legs up and braced her heels along the top of the door. Cool February air washed across her bare skin, making her all the more conscious of her vulnerable position.

"I taught you to come in my mouth."

He said the words against the inside of her knee and then kissed his way down her thigh, lowering himself to his knees in the process. "You were shy at first, and so nervous your legs trembled…just like now." Those wicked green eyes sent her a look of pure masculine satisfaction. "Nervous?"

She bit her lip, because she didn't know what might fly out of her mouth. *No. Yes. Please.* It was anyone's guess. The silence earned her a knowing smirk before he raked his teeth over delicate skin and sent a current of need straight to parts of her so overstimulated a wayward breath might leave her reeling. Her body jerked in reaction.

He laughed, but there was a surprising amount of affection in the sound, and the hands supporting the backs of her thighs swept up and down, soothingly. "You jumped every time I touched you then, too. Especially here…"

He kissed her. Right there. Dead on target, but just a fleeting brush of lips and a staggering gentleness that only strung her tighter. So tight she jerked again, damn him. A yearning moan vibrated from her chest—possibly her soul.

"Yeah, you took right to this, baby girl. Remember? Once I showed you what I could do, you forgot all about nerves, and shyness. I had you trembling all over, for different reasons, and begging me not to stop. Think you'll beg this time, too?"

"Fuck you."

"Fuck you, Sinclair."

And then he proceeded to, hard and fast, with lips, teeth, and—oh...ohhh—tongue. She fought it for one useless second, unwilling to let him win, but every lash whipped what promised to be a brutal orgasm to new urgency. The wet sound of his mouth working her filled the silence, punctuated by her panting breaths. Soon dignity surrendered to need. She chased it, one hand wrapped around the oh-shit handle, the other clenched in his hair. Somehow, she'd gotten one boot wedged into the corner where windshield met dashboard. His shoulder braced the other. Her jeans stretched tight between her ankles like an awkward tether. Just when she thought she couldn't take another hit, he closed his lips around her clit and applied devastating suction. Suddenly she was on the brink, quivering and whimpering in the face of agonizing pleasure.

And then—the bastard—he raised his head. Green eyes burned into hers. "Say it," he ordered.

She ground her teeth. "I hate you." She did. She hated him for leaving. Hated him for coming back. Hated how easily he'd gotten her across the front seat of his car, with her ass hanging out the door and her jeans around her ankles, about to burst into tears because she needed him so badly.

A hard palm smacked her unprotected ass. The sound sent a trio of birds flying from the tops of tall pines overhead. "That's for lying."

Another smack—not hard, but over the same stinging skin—and her nerve endings sang. "That's for putting this ass at risk by lighting out of the bus depot like a bat out of hell."

"I *hate* you."

Cool fingertips drifted over her still-tingling flesh, and she realized he traced his own handprint. The small discomfort didn't distract from the pounding ache between her legs. If anything, it only intensified the sensation.

"I missed you." Whether he was telling her, or prompting her, she didn't know, but the words fanned unfair places. Her whimpered response turned into a groan when his lips followed the path his fingers had outlined. That mouth. She needed that mouth…

"Shane, please—"

His lips drifted closer. "You know I love to hear you beg for it, Sinclair. I can't tell you how many times I've dreamed of you whispering, 'please,' in that breathless voice, and I wake up hard and hurting every damn time. Just as hard and hurting as I am now. But this time it's going to take more than please." With that, he moved to the other cheek and drew an intricate design with the tip of his tongue, seemingly content to torture her forever.

Hot, sweet misery overwhelmed her. Frustrated tears stung her eyes. She had two options. Tell him to go to hell and drag her miserable, needy ass inside along with the tattered remains of her pride, or…

"I hate you." She barely managed a whisper—one last act of defiance before she gave in to his demand. He heard her, and somehow, he knew he'd won. His tongue grazed her clit.

Her muscles gave out, and she fell back against the seat. The ceiling of the Rover blurred behind a haze of scalding tears. "I…" Oh, God, she was going to say it. "I m-missed you."

The words tore through her, annihilating boundaries she'd established and maintained for a decade, leaving her wide open and at his mercy.

But then he was there, giving her what she needed, rewarding her honesty with hard, thorough strokes. Staying with her as she bucked and shuddered. Staying with her as her fingernails raked his scalp and her broken cry clawed the air.

The last thing she heard before the shattering combination of pleasure and fear took over was her own voice repeating three words like a shameful confession.

"I…missed…you."

. . .

Victory raged through him, thundering like a heartbeat in time to her words. Damn right she'd missed him. He wasn't in this alone. The uncontrived truth in her voice couldn't be mistaken, and that kind of honesty deserved some serious positive reinforcement. After he saw her through this orgasm, he planned to flip her over, give her stubborn ass one last slap—to make sure she understood this wasn't just about old memories, this was about them here and now—and then reward them both for today's breakthrough with an exhaustive fucking ten years in the making.

He'd imagined her like this, on-and-off, for a decade, and even though he had a pretty good imagination, those fantasies made a pale substitute. Since the night of the wedding, however, imagination had escalated to cravings. A constant thirst he hadn't been able to quench…until now. He could spend hours here, drinking his fill, drowning in her, if she'd let him. But even as he gentled his kisses and slowed his tongue to the softest of caresses, her sobs increased.

That was new. Not the tears. She'd always been a crier. It had scared the shit out of him the first time, but she'd blushed and promised they weren't tears of pain, or sadness, they just…happened. Eventually, he'd realized if he made her come hard enough, she couldn't hold them back. Those tears of pleasure were beyond her control, but not *his*, and he considered them the sign of a job well done. Once her orgasm subsided, however, they always tapered off, which these showed no signs of doing. No, this was something else. Maybe pain? Maybe sadness? Hell, maybe her foot was stuck there in the crevice over the dash, but until he knew more, there would be no flipping, slapping, or fucking.

Instead, he eased away from the sweetest pussy he'd ever had the pleasure of plunging his tongue into. The familiar jut of her hipbone beckoned, and he bestowed a kiss there before running his lips over her fluttering stomach. Her leg had to come down before he could go any higher, so he hooked his hand under her thigh and lifted her knee toward her chin. Her foot slid out easily, and he lowered her leg to the seat. Sobs, now muffled by the arms she'd flung over her face, continued.

Okay. Not the foot.

He worked his way up the midline of her slender torso and nudged the poncho out of his way so he could press a kiss to the swell of her breast, directly over her heart. Her breath stopped, but then released on another small sob.

This was going to get tricky. He planted a knee on the seat, braced a forearm on the center console, and nuzzled the underside of her jaw. When he reached her ear, he deliberately teased the soft lobe, where he knew she was ticklish, and hoped for a laugh…a giggle. Anything. He got another shaky breath.

"There"—he kissed her salty lips—"that wasn't so hard now, was it?"

The sarcasm earned him a watery laugh. She'd always appreciated irony. He kissed her again, just to make sure she'd let him, and then drew her arms away from her face. First one, then the other, placing them on either side of her head.

"Christ, you're beautiful."

He got a choked laugh this time, though he'd been completely serious.

"I'm a mess." She sniffed and blinked at the ceiling. Then her chin trembled. "I'm sorry."

Fuck. This was going in the wrong direction. He grabbed a handful of her thick, cable-knit thing and backed out of the car, pulling her into a sitting position as he went. "You don't have anything to be sorry for. I made you a promise, and I didn't keep it. You deserved to know why. But you didn't owe me an explanation or a second chance, and you're entitled to your anger."

"No." She dropped her head into her hand and shook her head. "I'm not. I've been angry with you for so long, for stuff you don't even know about, because it was easier than facing…things."

He waited for her to elaborate, but apparently, she planned to leave it at that. No good.

"Sinclair?"

She looked up. "What?"

"Talk to me. It's time."

"Now?"

Had one word ever been more filled with reluctance? "Well, not this very instant, no. I appreciate this might not be a conversation we want to have while sitting in my car, with my dick hanging out and your pants around your boots." He backed up to give her room to scoot out of the car and promised his protesting cock they'd get back to the flipping, slapping, and fucking as soon as he could be damn sure the next time she cried in his arms it was for the right reasons. "Invite me in for coffee."

In what looked like one continuous move, she hopped down, grabbed her jeans, and shimmied them up her long legs. "If we're having this conversation, we're going to want something stronger than coffee."

Chapter Ten

Sinclair dropped two short tumblers and a half-empty bottle of whiskey onto her table with little regard for the glassware, but temper was wasted on the scarred pine. It had seen everything, survived everything, and accepted her carelessness with three soft *thunk*s.

Shane looked up at her from his seat on the other side of the table. "You're serious? It's not even noon."

"We were half naked in my driveway three minutes ago, and you're going to get scandalized over a pre-noon drink?" The lip of the bottle clinked against the rim the glass closest to him as she poured a double. The scent of charred oak and vanilla seared her nose.

"Come on, how bad can it be?"

In answer, she lowered herself into a chair and poured another two fingers of the aged-to-amber liquid into the second glass.

His lips twisted into a jaded smile. "Baby girl, I wrote this scenario before I even boarded the bus to Parris Island. You met someone over the summer. Some smooth-talking French guy swept you off your feet, and you forgot all about the screwup who had nothing going for him besides a shot at the Marines in lieu of a jail cell. You were so far beyond me by the time I was able to reach out, a part of me knew I'd already missed my chance."

Tempting. Oh, so tempting to go with his version of events. Write it off to his delay, and her fickle youth, and be done with it. No harm, no foul. But that wasn't what happened. There had been harm. She brought the glass to her lips and tossed back the shot in one long, burning swallow. After a moment, the burn subsided, but the fire lingered in her veins like a distant relative to courage. "I was pregnant."

He stared at her for a long moment, his face absolutely neutral, and then picked up his glass and took a long swallow. "What?"

"Before you start calculating ten years of child support payments, or judging me for whatever choice I made, you should know I lost the baby."

"I…" He broke off, looked away, and downed the rest of his drink.

Had she ever seen him speechless before? Not that she recalled. Compelled to fill the silence, she added, "Nobody knows this except my family."

He looked back at her. Unflinching. "I'm sorry."

The bone-deep sincerity in his words hit her like a body blow. She pushed back from the table quickly enough to cause a screech of chair legs over floorboards and struggled for a pat reply. "Me, too."

"How did it happen? I thought you were on the pill?"

I was stupid and reckless? "Darcy Briggs gave me her pills, because she'd broken up with her boyfriend. I didn't know I was supposed to wait forty-eight hours before I relied on them without backup. I was so anxious to give you the perfect birthday present, I didn't read the fine print."

He nodded slowly, as if digesting the information. "So, you think our first time…?"

"First or second. One of the earliest. Between you leaving, and then Savannah and me flying out to meet up with our cousins and backpack through Europe, I didn't realize. I missed you so much, Shane. Honestly, that gaping hole you left in my life took in all my attention. If not that, then the effort to walk around like a normal person and pretend the hole wasn't there."

"I know. I felt the same way. I'm sorry," he said again, and she shook her head to fend it off.

"By the time I got to Paris, I knew something was wrong. I taxed what little French I knew to buy a pregnancy test. When it read positive, I just…I don't know. I freaked. I tried to reach you by calling the base, but when the guy asked me to state the precise nature of the emergency, my throat froze. I hung up, boxed up all the careening emotions, and shoved them to the back of my mind. I told myself to sit tight until you called. Because I knew you'd call. You'd promised me you'd call as soon as you could."

"Sinclair—"

"But you didn't call." She was pacing like a boxer in a ring, but she couldn't get the story out if she stood still. "And we just kept moving. Frankfurt. Bonn. When we hit Rotterdam, I had really bad cramps, but I sucked it up. We'd figure everything out when we talked. Then we went to Amsterdam, and…"

She stopped stalking back and forth on her side of the table and poured herself another drink. This part took effort. Memories were flooding in faster than she could organize them. Long-buried feelings rode in their wake. Feelings she'd never really experienced until that summer. Fear. Panic. Helplessness. She took a sip and swallowed before continuing, "And in Amsterdam the pain flared into an overwhelming thing that I couldn't ignore. Savannah found me curled up on the bathroom floor in our hostel, feverish and bleeding. She called for help, and called our parents. I woke up in a hospital about twenty-four hours later, with my parents and a doctor hanging over my bed. I'd had an ectopic pregnancy that continued too long. The doctor spewed a lot of information—a congenital defect resulting in a weird curvature in the tube, so the pregnancy couldn't progress the way it should. I'm down to one now, but the defect was bilateral, so my chances of conceiving the normal way are, according to the surgeon, remote." And if she did, her chances of having another ectopic pregnancy were good.

"Fuck it, Sinclair." He braced his forearms on his knees and stared at the floor. "You should have let me know."

"Are you kidding me?" She drained her glass and put it on the table with an ill-tempered slam. "I didn't dare breathe your name. My parents were upset, to say the least." She dropped into her chair and then poured herself another shot. Thinking about everything that had happened up until this point—talking about it—emotionally drained her, but the next part? Whiskey-induced numbness might help her make it through without bawling.

"My father…" She closed her eyes and time traveled ten years back and a continent away. "My easygoing, fair-minded father was *livid*. My mom was surprisingly pragmatic about the whole thing. Sort of like, *Okay, this happened. We're going to get you well, get you home, talk about the mistakes you made that led to the situation, and then we're moving on*." Her mom's drama-free reaction could still wring a laugh out of her. "I mean, don't get me wrong, she grounded me for life, but very calmly. She went easy on me."

"And your dad?"

Shane's question came from across the table, but it might as well have been from anywhere. The memory pulled her so deeply into yesterday. She sighed, opened her eyes, and blinked her unknowing coconspirator into focus. "My father wanted the name of the guy responsible for knocking up his sixteen-year-old daughter and landing her in a hospital. He wasn't in the mood to go easy on anyone. Not on me, for violating his trust. Not on the guy who violated his daughter, for damn sure. If I had given him the vaguest clue it was you, your world would have turned to shit so fast your head would have spun."

She spun her empty glass on the table as an example. Restless hands.

Now he released a breath, looked up, and pinned her with a green gaze full of regret. "So, you didn't tell him."

It wasn't a question. No answer required, but something in those eyes made her speak. She spun the glass again. "I was a fool, not an idiot. I understood the implications of spilling my guts. You would have stood trial for statutory rape and possibly gone to jail. You'd have been booted out of the Marines. Your life would have been ruined."

He nodded and then got up and walked around the table. When he reached her, he crouched by her chair. A muscle ticked in his jaw, but other than the small sign of tension, she couldn't pinpoint his reaction.

"You must have been very angry with me by then. I hadn't called. I couldn't write. As far as you knew, I was some faithless asshole who'd kept none of my promises, and I was getting off without a single consequence while you paid for all our…"

She got the impression he considered and rejected the word "mistakes."

"…for everything." His eyes locked on hers. "I wouldn't have blamed you for speaking up, baby girl. I deserved everything your father had in mind. Why didn't you?"

"I told you why," she shot back, knowing she sounded defensive. "Ultimately everything that happened was my own fault. I brought it on myself by screwing up with the birth control. I compounded the screwup by falling for a guy who was leaving for boot camp as soon as he graduated. You weren't sticking around. I went into it with my eyes wide open."

He shook his head, rejecting her explanation. "I'd promised you I'd contact you, and I didn't. Couldn't, as it turned out, but you didn't know that. And still, you didn't speak up. Why?"

What the hell had her father done to her furnace? Why was it so hot in here? Needing air, and space, she started to push back from the table, but Shane caught the chair legs and held her in place. "Why didn't you tell him, Sinclair?"

"Shane, so help me God, I'm going to slap you again if you don't back off."

"Do it. I'll take any punishment you dish out, but I'm not backing off until you answer my question. Why. Didn't. You. Tell. Him."

Hot words scalded the back of her throat, burned there until she had to let them out. "Because I loved you, you bastard."

He cupped a hand to the back of her head and drew her down until her forehead rested against his. His warm, whiskey-laced breath flowed over her lips like some rare vintage. "I loved you, too, Sinclair. I loved you like I'd never loved anyone or anything in my whole pathetic life, and I wanted you so badly I never gave much consideration to the risks. Hell no, you didn't bring it on yourself. I was the adult —"

"Oh, please." She straightened. "You're a whopping year-and-a-half older than me, and the whole birthday seduction was my idea."

"I was eighteen. I had no right accepting that present from you."

"Did you honestly give our ages a thought at the time?"

"No, but that's on me, too. I should have. Add it to the shit-ton of things I should have done differently. If I hadn't been busy righteously fucking up my first attempt at adulthood, I would have been able to call you like I promised. I would have been there for you. It wouldn't have been *your* problem, it would have been *our* problem." He kissed her softly. "I'm sorry I let you down. I won't do it again."

The sincerity in his words shook her. She resorted to cynicism to combat the weakness. "Careful what you take on there, Shane. There's no need to pull the future into this. We've settled the past. Take that victory. It's a big one, because I've been angry with you for a decade. You weren't around to stick up for yourself, which made you my perfect personal scapegoat. Everything I didn't want to own, I shoved onto you. Ending up ashamed and afraid in an Amsterdam hospital? Shane's fault. Having to gain back my parents' respect? Shane's fault. Unsure my father would ever look at me the same again? Shane's fault."

He reached out a long arm and pulled the chair at the head of the table over. Then he sat, facing her, so they were knee-to-knee. "He loves you."

Leave it to him to laser in on the deepest wound. "Yes. He does. But I scared him. Disappointed him. Shook his view of me, and of himself. My mom had to spell it out for me, because I couldn't see past his anger, but she told me…" *Damn.* A lump lodged behind her vocal cords. She swallowed, but it stuck there. Her voice quavered from the effort of getting around it. "She told me he felt like a failure as a father."

"Sinclair—"

"No." She shook her head. "She wasn't being mean, she was explaining. My father considered protecting his girls one of his most important jobs. He did it in little ways, like putting training wheels on our bikes, or looking under our beds when he tucked us in at night to make sure there were no monsters, but also in big ways. He taught us to react if we felt threatened, and how to throw a punch without breaking our hands. He taught us to drive."

"You need a refresher course."

She laughed at his snide comment on her driving skills, despite the emotion clogging her throat. "He thought he'd done a pretty good job with all the protective dad stuff, until his sixteen-year-old daughter landed in a hospital, recovering from a miscarriage. He hadn't protected me from that. I hadn't let him."

"He felt helpless," Shane said quietly.

"He did. And by refusing to give him a name, I was compounding his helplessness. I wasn't letting him slay the dragon. It caused a rift. A big one."

"You bridged it?"

She swallowed hard. "We did. Eventually. I earned his trust again, not just as a daughter, but as a person. Plus, I got older, and less in need of protection. He wasn't on the hook for my safety and well-being anymore."

"Yeah. That's why he comes over to change your furnace filter, and you go to dinner every Sunday."

"Little gestures," she conceded, but his observation made her smile. His lips curved, too, lifting a degree higher on one side than the other in a sardonic, and ridiculously sexy, grin.

Then those lips straightened, and his gaze roamed her face before settling on her eyes with a steadfast resolve. "I'm going to earn your trust back, Sinclair."

• • •

Thick black lashes curtained Sinclair's eyes, but her lips tightened briefly in a fleeting frown. "There you go, talking in the future again." She leaned forward in her chair, resting her elbow on his shoulder as she brought her face closer to his. "We don't have a good track record for getting the future to play out the way we want. I prefer to concentrate on the here and now. Take this opportunity to work the leftover chemistry out of our systems."

Then her lips moved over his, warm and persuasive. Distracting, but no so much so he didn't recognize her effort to hijack the conversation and steer it away from plans… trust…anything that required her to rely on him. He wasn't going to let her do it. And she didn't really want him to, or he wouldn't be sitting here. She wouldn't have let him into the place she considered her fortress and sanctuary if all she sought was a clear conscience and a closure fuck. No, sir. This was a test. One he needed to pass…his thoughts drifted south as her hand slid purposefully up his inseam…or die trying.

Since passing meant demonstrating there was more between them than leftover chemistry, he caught those wayward fingers before they reached their destination. Being denied surprised her enough to have her abandoning the kiss and leveling an exasperated look at him. Oh, yeah, she wasn't accustomed to anyone putting on the brakes. He lifted her hand to his mouth, and bit the side of her thumb. "I'm not that easy. You can't just pour me a drink and grab my dick."

Her dark brows shot up. "Since when?"

"Since now. My dick. My rules. Show me around first."

Her brows came down, low enough to carve a little notch of consternation between them. "Another tour? I just downed three shots, Shane. I can't drive anywhere."

"Show me around *here*," he clarified then stood and pulled her to her feet. On his own, he crossed to the opposite end of the big, open room, where a drafting table and swiveling stool positioned beneath a skylight set off her studio space. Framed sketches of rings, necklaces, and other adornments decorated the walls, and he found himself appreciating the contrast of sparkling sophistication against the unpretentious backdrop of knotted boards. The contradiction offered a perfect reflection of the woman herself. Because she remained by the table, looking at him like he was full of shit, he added, "Come on. Let's see this woodpile you're so attached to."

She stared at him a second longer, trying to figure his game. Finally, she shrugged and crossed to him. "As I mentioned before, it's a work in progress."

And it was, but by the time she'd shown him around the main level, with its high ceilings and open layout, he could see the work she'd already done and visualize the end product. Her running commentary about walls becoming windows, original hand-hewn ceiling beams, and reclaimed floors helped. Admittedly, he wasn't a hearth-and-home kind of guy—he didn't, technically, have either—but by the time she finished showing him around the main floor, he could understand what she saw in hers. Standing for over a century and a half gave scarred boards and worn stone an honest integrity a newer build simply couldn't capture, but those walls also whispered with potential.

"When I get my permits," she said and gestured toward an old-fashioned spiral staircase fanning up to what had once been the hayloft, "I'll expand the upper level."

Yeah, "when," not "if." Clearly, she refused to contemplate any other outcome.

"Right now, there's only my bedroom, and a small bathroom. Anyway"—she faced him and did a little flourish with her hands—"that's it. The grand tour."

"You're not going to show me your bedroom?"

Her expression turned guarded, which gave him his answer before she responded. She really *wasn't* planning to let him see the inner sanctum—where she slept, and dreamed. Predictable, considering she didn't trust him, but even so, disappointment put a dull ache in his chest.

"No man who calls my home a woodpile gets to see my bedroom."

"That's awfully strict." He stepped closer.

Her chin lifted. "My bedroom, my rules."

He moved closer, backing her up until the heels of her boots hit the first stair. Then he lowered his mouth to her ear. "Has *any* man seen your bedroom?"

"That's none of your business."

So, no. His pulse kicked up. "What's the matter? You got something up there you don't want me to see? Were you maybe *thinking* of me this morning, and left your bed a wreck and a personal item on your nightstand?"

"Get over yourself," she tossed back, but she said it on a laugh, so he pressed forward, forcing her up a stair.

"Show me your bedroom."

"I'm not that easy."

For the first time in…ever, challenging her wasn't going to work. Fine. He could switch tactics. He kissed the corner of her mouth. "What if I apologized for the woodpile comment?"

Her eyelids drifted down, and her fingers curled into his belt loop. "I'd accept your apology, but my bedroom's still not on the tour."

He kissed the opposite corner and then raised his head. "What if I said I was wrong the other night, when I suggested you should take a buyout?"

Her eyelids flew open, and she stared up at him. "Really?"

"Yeah, really. You were right. You can't go a mile down the road and find the exact same thing you have here. A buyout won't work. This is too unique."

She tipped her head to the side, and her lips twisted into a half smile. "Nice to hear, but ultimately irrelevant. You don't make the decisions. You point out the risks and offer solutions." The smile disappeared, and she set her jaw. "It's on me to convince the city planning commission to grant my permit, and deny theirs."

She'd summed up the situation perfectly. This was her

problem to handle, but the look on her face reminded him too much of a girl outside a gym, about to take on a guy twice her size who didn't give a damn what she wanted. The impulsive part of him he no longer let handle executive functions wrested control of his prefrontal cortex. His hand curved around the nape of her neck and brought her face close to his. His mouth was running before he could shut it down. "I'll figure a way to work it out."

Her eyes widened. "What?"

"It's my job to find solutions, and I'm going to find one for you." Fuck if he knew how, but now that the words were out, he realized he meant them.

"But…I thought you favored the simplest option?"

"I said the simplest option usually wins the day. Governments especially tend to like the most economic solutions, but simple economics don't make something right. You bought the barn as a home, not an investment, and you shouldn't have to sacrifice your home because it's suddenly inconvenient for others. I'll come up with a solution. I promise."

"How…?"

"Just trust me," he repeated. Her lips parted on another question—one he probably couldn't answer—so he ended the conversation by commandeering her upper lip with his teeth. At her sigh of surrender, he dragged her up and into his arms, palming her ass through her jeans as she wrapped her legs around his waist. He carried her upstairs, but stopped on the landing outside the half-open door.

"Show me your bedroom, Sinclair." His voice held a note he didn't recognize. Desperation. He needed some gesture from her. Some privilege. Even a small one.

Teeth scoured the line of his jaw, and then her cool voice filled his ear.

"Only if you let me grab your dick."

A man who didn't know her as well might interpret the

retort as a sexy joke, but he knew her well. It was her way of establishing limits. Specifically, limiting the things bonding them together to sex. She was trying to set the terms.

Sorry, baby girl. No deal.

Yes, he was already kissing her. Already pushing through the door of her whitewashed bedroom. And yes, his hands were already under her shirt, bracketing her ribs and closing in on the lush weight of her breasts, but that wasn't any kind of surrender on his part. *His* plan involved making her need him—on more than just a temporary, physical level—but a resourceful man used any means at his disposal. Satisfying her physical needs was a means, and he intended to satisfy her until she couldn't think straight. He simply had to do it while enforcing one hard stop. He'd never been inside her without anything less than her absolute and total trust, and he refused to start now.

Details filtered in as he crossed the room—filmy white curtains covering dormer windows, the cushion of a rug beneath his feet, and…he stopped dead in his tracks. "Holy shit."

She actually blushed a little. "What? Just because I live in a barn, I can't appreciate a little luxury where I sleep?"

Centered under a soaring, multi-paned skylight sat a big, upholstered sleigh bed. It dominated the space, dove-gray velvet head and footboards gracefully rolled outward, practically inviting him to put them to use.

Impractical and romantic, just like the woman who spent her nights cradled in it. She owned up to her impractical side easily enough, but she tended to keep the romantic side under wraps. Or did she? Unjustifiably proprietary instincts had him asking questions he had no right to ask, and might not be prepared to hear the answers to.

"No other man has been in this room with you? In that bed with you?"

"You're the first," she admitted, breathing into his ear.

"Don't let it go to your head."

Oh, it went to his head, and a few other places. He rubbed his lips against hers and sat himself down on the edge of the bed so she straddled his lap. She deepened the kiss. Need and trust—the move felt a little like both. He'd take it. He gripped her hips and shifted her more tightly onto his lap. "I appreciate your honesty, Sinclair. Let's aim for some more. What we have here isn't leftover chemistry. Every single thing that's happened between us since I got back is new. You're not a sixteen-year-old with a wild streak and no sense of her own power. I'm not an impulsive fuckup skating through life by the seat of my pants."

He kissed her hard, to seal those words in her mind, before continuing. "I'm not that guy anymore. I'm going to prove it to you."

Slender arms wrapped around his neck. She tilted her head and angled her lips toward his mouth. "It doesn't matter. Nothing matters except this moment right now. No past. No future. Just this." It seemed she had her own points to prove, because she punctuated the assertion with a slow, sliding kiss.

He'd spent most of his adult life subscribed to the same theory, but it had never held true when it came to her, and it still didn't. Ten years had changed a lot for him, but not that. She mattered. What she thought of him mattered. There'd been a time when she'd thought enough of him to risk more than her body, and invest more than the moment directly in front of her. He'd had her trust, shared her dreams, and she'd shared his. Having her in his arms now without the rest of it felt like holding only half of her. He wanted all. He didn't have a fucking clue how he was going to get it, but he'd spent the last decade becoming a master at devising plans—complex, airtight plans that could hold up to any contingency—so he would damn well come up with a plan for her. For them.

And while he might not know every step he needed to

take yet, he knew the first one. Give her what she wanted, right here and now. He understood the underlying reason for her need, even if she didn't, and it had nothing to do with leftover chemistry. Confession might be good for the soul, but it was hell on the emotions, and wading through years of hurt and disappointment left her desperate to wash the ugly residue away in a flood of pure, fundamentally cleansing pleasure. She needed relief, and she wanted it from him.

Providing it, while not crossing the boundary he'd drawn for himself, might well kill him, but some missions were worth the risk. He broke the kiss and dragged her poncho over her head. It landed in a heap on the rug, and he pulled in a breath. She sat there in a snug white top suspended by thin straps that looked like they'd snap with one good tug. The nearly sheer cotton did little to hide the swells of her breasts, or the tight, gravity-defying points inspiring his cock to gravity-defying feats of its own. Between the night at the Lookout and their driveway adventures, his mouth and hands had appreciated the enhancements Mother Nature had bestowed to her body, but now his throat dried in anticipation of finally being able to look his fill.

"Off." He growled, afraid he'd rip the thing away if he touched it. "I want to see you."

She swept it over her head in one graceful pull, arching her back in the process. He stopped her right there, with her arms crossed over her head. Her shirt dangled around her wrists. Her elbows pointed to the sky, her tits lifted toward him like a gift.

Same pale, silky skin and pretty pink tips, but they were fuller now. More opulent. "Don't move." He blew the instruction across one straining peak, a shade deeper than he remembered, and watched it draw tighter. Her thighs clenched his hips, and a tormented little moan drifted to his ear. The entire continuum of heaven and hell in one small sound.

"I want to see you, too," she said, managing to infuse a good dose of imperious southern demand into her unsteady voice. Then she took it upon herself to pull her arm free from the white top and run her hand down his chest, under his sweater, along his abs.

Heat burned through him from every point of contact and shot directly to his pounding cock. Okay, her touching him was a luxury he couldn't afford, or he'd be buried deep inside her before his head had time to remind his dick that wasn't the plan.

"Not yet." He caught her roving hand, drew both of them behind her back, and gave the stretchy top still dangling from her other hand a tug. Perfect. Strong enough to do the job, but soft enough not to cut into her. A quick series of twists, and he secured her wrists.

"What the…?" She automatically tried to pull an arm free, but the bind held. Her eyes darkened as she realized what he'd done, then flashed at him. "Hey."

"Trust me." He kissed her again, to end the debate before it started, and did his level best to issue a promise with every part of his mouth. He kept at it until her shoulders relaxed and her chest heaved.

"Shane—" she started as soon as he raised his head.

"You wanted to see me." He bent his arm behind his head, took a handful of his sweater, and yanked it off. That, too, momentarily distracted her from the argument. Her gaze bounced all over him—throat, shoulders, chest…lower—and he caught himself tightening every hard-earned muscle to keep her captivated. Eventually her gaze lifted to meet his. He saw a gratifying fever in those midnight-blue depths.

"I want to touch you," she said bluntly.

"Not this time, baby girl."

Her chin jutted, and he nearly grinned at the familiar, stubborn gesture. Sinclair hated being told no. Even when it was for her own good.

She also knew how to change tactics on a dime. Like now. She raised one dark brow and lifted the corner of her mouth in a seductive smile. "Used to be you loved having my hands on you. I touched you everywhere." She leaned forward until her mouth grazed his ear and murmured, "Everywhere… remember?"

Hell, yes, he remembered. Every second of every single moment she'd had her hands on him was etched in his memory. From the way her palm had rested tentatively on his cheek during that first "thank you" kiss—and unlocked some better side of his character just by acknowledging his reckless heroism—to the no-holds-barred explorations her curious fingers had taken those times she'd cradled his cock in her mouth and driven him right out of his motherfucking mind.

"I remember everything. I want all of it, and more, but if I let you put your hands on me right now, I'm not going to be able to do the things I want to do to you."

Her eyebrows lifted. "Exactly what do you want to do to me?"

She might have been aiming to intimidate him with that look, but he wasn't easily intimidated. The fact that she'd try made him want to haul her up and fuck her senseless, but instead, he ran his hands up her arms and pulled her toward him until her breasts swung forward and their sweet weight landed against his chest. Over her soft moan, he said, "I'm going to have my way with you, Sinclair. And I'm going to whip you into such a frenzy, you won't give damn how I do it."

Slowly, he lifted her, dragging her tits over his chest. Her moan got louder, and her eyelids fluttered. He repeated the move, holding her a little closer this time, increasing the friction. Her head fell back. "More."

"Once more." He switched his hold to her hips. "One more time, and then I use my mouth."

Her moan might have been agreement, or protest, but she widened her knees to press her center firmly against him. He pulled his abs taut to give her a good ride and lifted her again, closing his eyes to enjoy the scrape of her hard, hot nipples across his skin and the damp heat seeping through her jeans. This time he just kept going, and once he had her up there, tits level with his face, he closed his mouth around one tight peak. She gasped and jerked back a little, but that's really all she could do. He had her hips lifted, her hands tied, and she'd twined her legs around the chair to keep her lower body anchored to him. It wasn't until he drew her deeper, and she sucked in a breath, that it occurred to him she might be sore from the way he'd gone at her earlier.

"Too rough?"

"I like the way it hurts. Don't stop."

Not a chance, but it was time to remind her he could be careful, too. There'd been a time when he'd been very, very careful, and she'd liked it very, very much. He gentled his mouth. Her incoherent murmurs were the payoff for every soft kiss, every light flick of his tongue, and every ounce of his restraint.

When her fidgeting turned restless, and her breaths edgy, he reinforced his grip on her ass and stood. The move surprised a small cry out of her—and forced her into another trust-building exercise, given she was essentially a passenger in his arms. He strode to the end of the bed and set her down on the tufted velvet. A little nudge tipped her back and forced her to brace herself on her hands. He skimmed his palms down worn denim and tugged one boot off, then the other.

"Hurry," she said, and scooted toward him. "I want you. Now."

She couldn't possibly know what a picture she made, sitting there bared and bound on her princess bed, issuing orders like she had all the power in the current dynamic. In truth, she did, because this was him proving himself to her, but part of the proof involved getting her to have faith in him to give her what she needed, rather than what she asked for. He pulled her off the perch, nearly groaning at the way her breasts bounced from the impact of her feet hitting the floor, and then stepped close. "Patience, baby girl."

Her chin came up a notch. "I've never been known for my patience."

No, she hadn't. At eighteen he'd had the reputation for being impulsive, but she'd been the one to set the breakneck pace of their relationship. He'd been too young, and frankly, too far gone, to even think of slowing things down. But he wasn't an undisciplined teenager anymore. He hooked his fingers into the front of her jeans, and undid the button.

"It's time you learned some." Then, very slowly, he drew the zipper down. Even more slowly, he eased his hands into the now-gaping waist and pushed the denim over her hips. The jeans settled around her calves. He took a deliberate step back and paused to drink in the sight of her in tiny white panties. "I don't appreciate being rushed." To underscore the statement, he ran a fingertip along the edge of the silk, taking a lazy path from her hip to where the whisper-thin fabric disappeared between her thighs.

"I don't appreciate being tortured."

The ragged accusation made him smile. Same old Sinclair. "Torture? I haven't even looked at you yet."

Five full seconds of silence met that statement, followed by, "Okay, you've looked. Now undo my hands, and—"

He spun her around.

"Hey!"

"I'm not done looking." He swept her hair over her shoulder and pressed a kiss to the nape of her neck. "Not nearly done."

She twisted her hands, testing the makeshift restraint holding them together behind her back. "Shane…"

He laid a hand over her tethered wrists and placed another kiss between her shoulder blades. "Shhh. I'm busy looking." Then he spanned a hand along the base of her neck, and, keeping hold of her wrists, bent her over the bed. A line of white silk pulled tight between her ass cheeks.

"*Shane.*"

"Busy," he reminded her and kissed the small of her back, the *V* of her thong, and then he dropped to his knees and followed the path of the panties with his tongue.

"Oh…God. That's not looking. You don't look with your tongue."

"The Marines trained me to use all my senses to get a complete picture. Sight"—he hooked his fingers into the fabric stretched across the top of her ass and peeled the panties down—"touch"—he slid his palms along the smooth curves, parting them to get a better view of all his targets. Her fingers opened and closed above his head.

"Don't even…" She tried to squirm away but he held fast.

"Taste," he finished over her protest and swept his tongue from the last notch of her spine to the hot, slick flesh he'd exploited when he'd had her splayed out in the front seat of his car. She jumped and wiggled, but ultimately submitted with a defenseless sound. He drew back, slid a hand down her leg, and guided her knee up until he had it braced on the footboard. The position spread her thighs wide. The sight of her, open and ready for him, sent powerful mandates from primitive parts of his brain. He sat back on his heels, closed his eyes, and gave himself a crucial moment to fortify his resolve.

Sinclair, apparently, didn't have a moment in her. "Enough. You've looked your fill."

He pulled air into his lungs, let it out slowly, and waited for the pounding in his cock to subside from agonizing to merely brutal. When he was sure he had himself under control, he opened his eyes. "You're right. Enough looking.

Now I reintroduce my mouth to you properly."

Her forehead hit the bed with a soft thump. "Shane…"

Not a "no," so he ignored his name on her lips, angled his head, and got to work. The room filled with the sound of him making good on his promise. Her breathing turned heavy, each exhale accompanied by increasingly frustrated moans. She couldn't hold still, but he didn't try too hard to stop the jerky motions of her hips since most of her effort went into pushing herself into the path of his tongue.

Finally, those moans pitched up into a sharp curse. She tightened her hips and struggled to pull herself upright, but he put a stop to that by nudging her just enough to overbalance her.

The comforter muffled her next curse, and then she managed to turn her head and hit him with a look of pure, sweet desperation. "For the love of *God*, Shane. I can't take any more. I need you inside me. Now."

"I want to be inside you. Make no mistake. I'm suffering like the damned right now. My balls ache. My cock's throbbing and furious from neglect. But that's how it's going to stay because I don't earn the privilege of being inside you until I earn your trust."

An aggrieved moan was her only response. He rested one hand along the top off her ass, just below her tightly clenched fists, and rimmed her swollen threshold. "Don't worry. I won't allow you to suffer while I'm proving myself. I'll make sure you come. Long, hard, and as many times as you can handle. Do you trust me to do that for you, baby girl?"

Then he plunged two fingers into her damp, hot channel, and her body answered for her. She arched off the mattress as the first spasm gripped her, and her uncensored scream of gratitude battered the old barn walls.

Maybe it wasn't an unqualified declaration of trust, but it was definitely a start.

Chapter Eleven

Shane shoved his rolled shirt cuffs up his forearms and checked his watch as he made his way across the open expanse of land once valued for its ability to produce cotton. Now the value took a different form—as the future site of the Whitehall Resort Golf Course.

As testament to that, two of the three engineers from the company Haggerty had retained to do the water report set up survey equipment by the creek bank. The third stood in deep conversation with Ricky Pinkerton.

Shit. He quickened his strides. Mayor Campbell expected him at a meeting across town with the developers of a subdivision, and after that, he had a flight to catch. His schedule didn't really allow for this unscheduled stop, and the engineers didn't need him looking over their shoulders, but he didn't want Ricky attempting to direct the scope of the project or the outcome.

The head of the team looked up from his tripod-mounted laptop and spotted him. The middle-aged engineer disengaged from Ricky and ambled over, saving Shane some extra steps.

He carried a Spectra Ranger data collector in his hand, and a well-worn utility belt around his waist held other tools of the trade. Someone accustomed to field work, Shane deduced, as the man extended a hand and introduced himself as Raj Patel. "Nice to meet you, Mr. Patel. Did Jack Haggerty explain our concerns?"

Ricky trailed the engineer, like a pissy shadow in his ugly yellow sweater. "I was just giving Raj here the overview, and explaining that the creek never floods."

"That's not true—"

The older man held up a hand. "Three things, as I understand. You are seeking confirmation of this land around the creek as a flood fringe"—he glanced at the creek as he spoke, then back to Shane—"and wanting to know how extensive the bank fortifications should be to prevent spillover. Lastly, you wish to understand how the fortification will affect the water level downstream."

"That sums it up," Shane agreed. "Any preliminary impressions?"

"Well, we are definitely standing in a flood fringe. You don't need a hydraulic study to tell you that. The topography speaks for itself."

"Yeah." He couldn't help shooting Pinkerton a "fuck you" look. "That's what I thought."

"Okaaay." Ricky rolled his eyes. "Never mind that the creek hasn't flooded in longer than anyone can remember, how high do we have to go to convince the city to issue the permit for the golf course?"

Fine. Pinkerton wanted to cut to the chase? They'd cut to the chase. "Assuming they fill the fringe up here to get the full half-foot leeway, what happens downstream?"

Raj shook his head. "Filling up here widens the floodway there." He gestured down the slope, toward the tree-line, and, ultimately, Sinclair's barn. "Narrow, shallow creeks like this

one can sustain only so much influx. One good rain, and..."
He widened his hands to demonstrate. "Luckily, Mr. Pinkerton
informs me there aren't any developments along the lower
portion of the creek, and so long as none are planned..." He
trailed off and shrugged.

Careful, Shane cautioned himself. The city wasn't paying
for a survey to help save Sinclair's barn, and Haggerty would
chew his ass if he got wind of Shane having a personal agenda.
"Mr. Pinkerton's statement isn't accurate, which he's well
aware of, but for the sake of argument, let's say downstream
development is part of the plan — "

"It's not part of the plan," Ricky inserted.

"Hypothetically speaking," Shane continued, ignoring
Ricky. "What would it take to do it safely?"

Raj puffed his cheeks and let the air out in a gust. "Lots
of money. Fortifying these banks up here is not such a big
deal. Negligible cost or environmental impact in shifting dirt
around. No interruption to the natural course of the creek.
Diverting the water flowing downstream, conversely, means
installing drains, aqueducts — "

"No fucking way," Ricky said. "The resort's not paying for
that. Not for one lousy barn. Neither is the city. I'll say it again
for the hard of hearing. The creek never floods."

"Because it widens up here," Shane bit out. "It won't
after you fortify." His gut tightened. The ill-advised promise
to Sinclair echoed in his brain. He gave Ricky his back and
directed another question to Raj. "What about for a very
small diversion, like, for a house or two?"

The engineer shook his head. "The size of the development
doesn't change the basic solution. Whether to avoid one
structure or a thousand, the water needs to go somewhere
else. Frankly, only a large development would warrant the
investment."

"You got that right," Ricky chimed in from behind

him. "And a large development won't happen as long as my grandmother's alive. I've heard enough. I'm done here. We're talking fairytales now."

Ricky strutted off. Fuck. Shane tugged at his tie, trying to relieve the noose-like tightness around his neck. A trickle of sweat slid between his shoulder blades. "What about managing the water upstream?" He was grasping at straws now, but he didn't have any other ideas.

"Ah. Well, then, you would be talking about a dam, and that requires a suitable reservoir area. Assuming such an area exists and could be secured for the purpose, you would also need a permit to build the dam, to impound water, and, perhaps more dauntingly, a shift in public opinion. Outside of farming communities, people dislike dams. Necessary permits might prove very challenging."

"What about…?" No alternative sprang to mind. Meanwhile, seconds ticked off in his brain. He needed to get going or he'd be late meeting the mayor, which wouldn't earn him any points. *Face it. This isn't going to get solved today.*

Obviously, Raj agreed, because he held up a hand to halt the conversation. "Mr. Maguire, we would be happy to draw up an addendum to the contract for the engineering of a water-management solution, but that's a longer, more involved assignment. I understood you wanted the report as soon as possible."

"I do." He needed to back off and let this guy do his job. There was still time. The report would take six weeks, and then the city planning commission would have to meet and review the findings. Somewhere between now and then, he'd come up with a viable solution. He had to.

• • •

"How was Tahiti?" Sinclair held the phone to her ear and

glanced at the clock over the stove. Her stomach gave a stupid and totally uncharacteristic flutter as she read the time. Shane was due any moment for tour number four. "Dress for a hike," was all he'd told her yesterday when he'd called.

"Three words," Savannah replied, sounding relaxed, replete, and possibly a little smug. "Over. Water. Bungalow."

"I trust you were naked the entire time?"

"I'm still naked. Are you still planning to be in Atlanta next month for the jewelry expo?"

Definitely smug. "Yes, but I'm not coming for dinner afterward unless you put some clothes on. The honeymoon's over." She peeked through her sheer curtains at her empty driveway.

"Oh, Sinclair," her sister sighed, "as long as Beau's got a pulse and a tongue, the honeymoon's never over."

She let the curtain drop back into place and grinned, despite her nerves. "I'm scandalized, Mrs. Smith-Montgomery. But it sounds like you had fun, and you weren't sick the entire time."

"I'm not going to lie to you. First trimester is not the ideal time to go on a snorkel boat."

"So noted, although I don't think it's going to be a problem for me. All's well on the baby front?"

"Yep. Baby likes the beach, as it turns out."

"Convenient, since mommy likes the beach." She paced over to her drafting desk and started straightening sketches.

"What can I say? He's his mommy's boy."

She stopped tidying. "Boy?"

"Yes." Savannah took an audible breath. "We just found out today. We've got a healthy baby boy in the works. I know I said I'd be thrilled either way, and I would, but—"

"But a boy is wonderful," Sinclair finished for her sister and gave fate an invisible high five. Beau had lost his first wife and their four-month-old daughter in a car accident a couple years before Savannah had moved into the apartment beside his. Falling in love again, the baby…all of it had been an emotional minefield for him. Having a baby boy was a completely new experience for both of them. Something solely theirs, that they didn't have to share with the past.

"Mom and Dad don't know yet," Savannah added.

"They won't hear it from me."

"Thanks. Mom's next on my call list. You don't have to keep it to yourself long." Savannah sighed. "So…what's new with you?"

"Me?" Was it her imagination, or did this sound like more than a casual inquiry on her sister's part? "Not too much. A national retailer expressed interest in carrying some of my pieces, and I picked up a few hefty new custom commissions."

"Sounds like you're kicking ass professionally, but to be honest, I'm more curious about your personal life. What's new there?"

Yep, Savannah was definitely chasing after specific information, and she'd studied at the knee of a master. She could be single-minded when she wanted to be, like a shark chasing prey. "Why do you ask?"

"I saw you dirty dancing with Shane Maguire at the wedding—"

"We were not dirty dancing. It was just a dance. One dance."

"I gave him your purse, and then the both of you disappeared, so in my book, it wasn't just a dance. You were wearing a different dress when you came back to the reception, which leads me to believe the escapade involved him tearing your clothes off."

"I didn't leave with him. There was no escapade. Jeez. Is that what everyone thinks? I couldn't keep my hormones under control through my own sister's wedding? He's an old friend. He happened by while I was having a problem with my dress and helped me out. I drove myself home and changed. Now you have the whole sordid story."

"That's not the whole story, and we both know it," Savannah said gently. "He's the guy, isn't he?"

Shit. She released a breath and rubbed her chest. "Yes."

"Does he know?"

"He does now." As briefly as possible, she explained their deal, and how that had evolved into…whatever it had evolved into.

"Wow," Savannah said when she finished. "So, what now?"

"I don't know," she answered honestly. "He wants a second chance and says he plans to stick around, but…" She walked over to the window again.

"You don't believe him?"

"I don't know." She was becoming the queen of I-don't-knows. "I'm not the kind of girl men stick around for—"

"Bullshit." The gentleness disappeared from Savannah's voice. "He didn't stick around. He couldn't, and deep down you know that, but since then you haven't let anyone get close enough to stick. I can name two reasons why that's the case, but neither has anything to do with you not being sticky enough."

"Okay, fine. Maybe I'm not looking to get stuck? I know this might be hard to believe, but if you look past the glow of your own happiness, you'll see a whole bunch of people—me included—who prefer casual, non-stick arrangements."

"How would you know what you prefer? You got hurt once. Things took an unplanned turn, and you got in way over your head. The experience left a scar. I understand. But you've been guarding yourself ever since. You're not sixteen anymore. You're a grown-ass woman. And a grown-ass woman knows how to handle a relationship without getting in over her head."

"You sound just like Mom."

"She's astute, our mother. But I bet even she doesn't have a clue as to the other reason you've avoided handing your heart to anyone again. It's because—"

"Why is it that everyone who gets into a serious relationship suddenly becomes an expert on love?" The heart in question started to pound, but she mustered up a laugh. "Henpecked single people everywhere want to know."

Savannah went on as if she hadn't interrupted. "You haven't given your heart to anyone else because the best parts of it are already spoken for. Shane has them. He's always had them."

"That's not true." She forced another laugh, which came out hollow because her lungs refused to hold air.

"Whether you like it or not," her sister insisted.

"I *don't* like it." The words flew out of her mouth, loud and angry, and not at all the outright denial she'd intended. She dropped down in a chair at her kitchen table and rested her forehead in her hand. "I don't like it," she repeated, letting the underlying truth settle over her. "Shit. What am I going to do?"

"He wants a second chance, Sinclair. You both deserve that much."

The sound of tires rolling up her driveway propelled her into motion. She got up and crossed to the door. "There's so much baggage between us." A lift of a handle, a hard tug, and the big door rolled open. She stepped out onto the stone porch and pulled the door shut behind her with a bang. The Range Rover rolled to a stop just a few feet away. "What if it doesn't work out?"

"What if it does?"

"Spoken like a newlywed."

Shane came around the front of the Rover, all masculine grace and rangy muscles in a black Henley and army-green utility pants. The late-afternoon sun put copper highlights in his uncharacteristically windblown hair, but the thing that really made her knees go weak was his face. A good day's worth of stubble lined his jaw, and the look in his eyes suggested she could expect to feel the rasp of it on every inch of her skin.

"Gotta go," she mumbled in the general direction of her phone and hit disconnect a moment before two strong arms pulled her up against the hard bluff of his body and a hot mouth covered hers.

Chapter Twelve

He'd meant to clean up and arrive on her doorstep looking a little less like he'd been running his ass off for the better part of forty-eight hours. But a quick shower and change of clothes had been the best he could manage, because he'd gone and done something impulsive—something besides haul her into his arms and take possession of her mouth as if he could suck every doubt out of her head with a long, thorough kiss—and ended up scrambling to get the details of a new plan in place.

Sadly, that plan didn't involve delivering orgasms in her driveway, so he ended the kiss in stages, cupping her jaw, brushing his mouth over hers, lingering there for increasingly brief moments until she sighed against his lips and opened her eyes. "You're late."

He was. Five minutes. "You're strict." He kissed her again, hard and quick. "You can punish me. Later."

One dark brow arched. "Careful what you promise, Maguire. I might hold you to it."

As she spoke, she rubbed her palm over his cheek, and it occurred to him she'd never seen him unshaven before.

At least not since going without a shave for more than a day made any discernable difference. Did she like it? He sure as hell liked the feel of her hand smoothing his jaw. "I'm at your mercy, once we're through with today's tour." He took her hand and led her to the car.

"Speaking of which, what *is* on this afternoon's itinerary?" She halted by the passenger door and tucked her phone into the pocket of her black, insulated ski vest. "Am I dressed right?"

He used the question as an excuse to inspect her, from the top of her sexy, bundled-up hair to the toes of her black-and-gray cross-trainers. True, he got a little caught up in the way her white thermal top clung to her breasts, but not so distracted he didn't consider if it would keep her warm enough once the sun set. Probably, but he could if it didn't. He opened the passenger door. "That works."

"Great." She climbed into the Rover, unknowingly treating him to a glimpse of long legs and her perfect, heart-shaped ass in skintight black leggings. Would she notice he'd only answered one of her questions?

As soon as he settled himself behind the wheel, she asked, "Where are we headed?"

That would be a yes. He reversed into a turn. "On a hike. Nothing too grueling."

"Okay, fine. But *where*?"

"One of the new subdivisions. You'll see." There was no way to divulge their exact destination without divulging more than he wanted her to know.

Apparently going with the flow suited her this afternoon, because she just rolled her eyes and then combed the side of his hair with her fingers. "Looks like you had a busy day."

He leaned into the rake of her nails against his scalp as she tried to bring order to hair he'd let wind dry after his shower because he hadn't wanted to spare extra minutes to run a comb through it. "A busy couple days," he admitted as he made the turn onto the main road. "I had a meeting in Virginia this morning with a special consultant, after coming off a full day of meetings yesterday." Not to mention a shitload of personal business he'd sprung on himself in his effort to give her tangible evidence he was invested in this.

She scoured her nails along the back of his neck and sent a scalp-tightening chill of pleasure along his nerve endings. Only the fact that he sat behind the wheel of a moving vehicle prevented him from dropping his head and giving himself over to those roaming fingers. "Sounds important."

"Hmm." Her fingertip brushed his earlobe, and his cock twitched. "Some of it is. Some is bullshit. Politics. Money. Jockeying for position."

"You thrive on the challenge." Her hand retreated down his neck and across the top of his shoulder.

"I like it, most of the time," he acknowledged. "I know it might seem counterintuitive, based on the guy I was until Uncle Sam got ahold of me, but I'm good at what I do. The planning, the logistics, and especially the execution. Acquiring those skills forced me to learn patience and get a handle on my reckless tendencies."

Then again, he'd let his impulsive side off the leash in a major way over the last forty-eight hours. He glanced her way to find her giving him a hard-to-read look. "I know a lot of people around here expected me to end up like Derek. Can't say I'm sorry to disappoint them."

She skimmed her fingers along his jaw, just a fleeting touch, and then lowered her hand to her lap. "I'm proud of you," she said quietly. "I always have been."

Something in his chest warmed and expanded, but he simply took her hand, joined their fingers, and gave her a smile. "Always? Why Sinclair, have you been keeping track of me?"

She shrugged. "I might have heard a thing or two, from time to time. Mrs. Pinkerton's cousin-in-law has a neighbor whose nephew works in the same nursing home where your mom works—or something like that. I'm never one hundred percent on her sources, but she seemed to know about every stripe and commendation, and then every promotion when you went private."

"No personal curiosity on your part, then?"

She shrugged again. "I might have visited the Haggerty website once or twice over the years."

"Just keeping tabs?"

Her smile dug a little indentation in her cheek. "Checking to see if you'd gotten fat and bald."

He laughed. "Disappointed?"

"Extremely."

"Well, I didn't have Claudia Pinkerton supplying me with highlights from the adventures of Sinclair Smith, but I cyberstalked you, too, from time to time."

"To see if I'd gotten fat and bald?"

He laughed and slowed to make a turn onto a narrow paved road. "To watch you establish your business, and grow it. I'm proud of you, too, baby girl." He gave her hand a squeeze and then released it to take the wheel and steer the Rover as the road transitioned from paved to dirt. "You turned something you loved into a successful career. That takes talent and hustle."

The road turned bumpy, but he risked a glance at Sinclair and found her blushing.

"Thank you," she said. "There's luck involved, too. I got some good visibility early on thanks to a sorority sister who married into a high-profile family. She asked me to design her rings and the jewelry she wore for the wedding. That parure I did for her is what really launched me."

"You can't underestimate the appeal of a good puh-roo."

What the fuck was a puh-roo?

"You don't have the faintest idea what I'm talking about, do you?"

She had him there. He could distinguish a ring from a necklace, but despite checking her website and social media posts, he didn't know much about jewelry. Given everything he had on deck for this evening, he figured he might as well tell the truth. "Honestly, the entire time I stalked you I was only on the lookout for one thing."

"Discount codes?"

"A change to your last name."

She stilled. "You checked to see if I'd gotten married?"

He braked and eased the Rover to a stop at the end of the dirt road. Resting his wrists on the wheel, he turned to her. "Back in the day, when you wouldn't answer my calls and returned my letters, my CO advised me I had no business trying to stay in contact with a sixteen-year-old girl who clearly wasn't feeling reciprocal. He told me to consider you the one that got away and let you get on with your life. I did, because a part of me had always figured it was only a matter of time before I fucked us up, and then—big surprise—I did, and obviously, you wanted nothing to do with me. But another part of me knew better. I ignored it. I shouldn't have."

She shook her head. "It's ancient history, Shane—"

He opened his door to cut her off, because he didn't want her to tell him it didn't matter. Their history mattered, and tonight was about proving it to her. "We're here. Ready to hike?"

. . .

Sinclair followed Shane past a sign announcing lots for sale, onto a parallel path of hard-packed dirt carved from the tracks of vehicles. Despite the evidence of human encroachment, vines wove around the trunks of mature trees and grew thick on either side of the trail. Back in high school, there had been no clear-cut walkway. No generous lots demarked by FOR SALE or SOLD signs and corner-staked with little orange flags. It had been untouched woodland. These days, it no doubt merited Shane's professional interest as one of Magnolia Grove's newest future home sites. Did he remember following her into these same woods on a sultry May night to celebrate his eighteenth birthday?

Somewhere around here grew a willow tree with limbs that reached the ground and had provided the perfect shelter for her to give him gifts she couldn't take back. Despite how everything between them had played out, she counted that night as one of the most special moments of her life. They were traipsing dangerously close to that sacred ground. The path veered, and she followed him around a bend. They walked past a fenced-off lot where a crew had assembled the frame of a large, two-story home. Her heart sank. Was the tree even around anymore? She didn't want to sully the memory of that night with some haphazard tour of new construction.

"How much farther?" she asked when the path split again. Another half-built house came into view, along with some NO TRESPASSING signs. Nothing looked familiar. She was all turned around.

"Let's go this way." He stopped at one of the orange flags staked into the ground near a narrow opening between two pines and held some branches aside for her.

She hesitated. "The sign says 'No Trespassing.'"

His slow smile belonged to an eighteen-year-old renegade. "There was a time when you were down for a little rule-breaking."

Maybe he did remember. "Yeah, but we're not kids anymore, and it wouldn't look good for the city's expert consultant to get busted for trespassing."

The smile only widened, carving a groove beside his mouth. "Trust me, baby girl." With that, he walked through the opening and disappeared behind the fringy overgrowth.

She danced with uncertainty for a moment. A woman who lived in the middle of nowhere knew her way around the wilderness, but they'd taken one too many turns while she'd been journeying down memory lane. The result? She wasn't sure how to get back to the car. She did know the region was blessed with a variety of wildlife that hunted at dusk and might not be intimidated by a lone woman on an empty trail—raccoons, foxes…skunks. Something skittered in the roots near her feet. "Shane!" She dived through the opening in the pines, only to run into an unyielding wall of muscle and bounce off with a breathless, "Oomph."

Quick hands caught her arms and steadied her. "It's official. Something about this place makes you want to jump me."

And that's when she saw it—lights shining from under the rounded, drooping branches of a winter-bare willow tree. Their tree. Taller, broader, but theirs. Her heart stuttered. "Shane?"

He took her hand and led her along a grassy expanse toward the willow. "Remember?"

How could she forget? The lantern light glowed, telling her he'd not only planned to bring her here, he'd taken time to set the scene, but suddenly, she didn't want to move. This spot held a special place in her heart, but it wasn't theirs. It never had been. And coming back now, weaving through property markers and signs, only underscored the fact. "This is beautiful"—she gestured toward the tree—"but we can't. There are laws. We don't belong here."

He turned to face her, but continued an unhurried backward walk toward the tree, pulling her with him. "We do. It's mine."

His words careened around in her head like bats, fast and hard to get a lock on. It's mine. It's. Mine. "What?"

"I bought the lot," he said and held a curtain of willow aside to usher her into the cloistered space beneath. A red-and-black plaid blanket covered the ground, and an insulated backpack anchored one corner.

Her ribs shrank, forming a painfully tight cage around her heart. "Why?"

For the first time all night, he looked uncomfortable. "The day before yesterday, I was out here for a meeting. While Campbell and I looked over the map of parcels for sale in the subdivision, I realized this lot was up for grabs. Somebody would buy it. Build a spec house, or their dream house, or whatever. Maybe they'd remove the tree. Maybe not. It was none of my business. I spent half a second trying to bullshit myself into believing I didn't care. I don't have deep roots anywhere—and most of the time I'm okay with that—but not this time." He looked down at the blanket, and she followed his gaze, practically seeing the ghosts of their former selves tangled together under the same encompassing limbs. "This place is important me. I needed to protect it."

She braced a hand on the tree trunk and immediately remembered leaning against it, raising her lips for his kiss. "I… Wow. I don't know what to say."

He took a step toward her. "Say you forgive me, for not protecting you."

Warning sirens blared in her head. He was merging past and present again, and it made a risky combination. Savannah's words came back to haunt her. *You haven't given your heart to anyone else because the best parts are already spoken for.*

All the parts of her heart she still held a claim to raced—trying to make a getaway. Instead she sagged against the tree. "Don't…"

"Don't what?" He stopped his slow advance. "We talked about what happened, now let's settle it. You won't trust me with your future until you forgive me for the past, and I'm not satisfied calling this a nostalgia fuck, and nothing more. Screw that, Sinclair. I want more. So do you. Trust me enough to forgive me for letting you go."

She didn't consider herself a cowardly person, but she battled a flight instinct so strong she actually visualized herself turning and running. Nothing lurking in the woods could be nearly as dangerous as the man in front of her, giving life to all her hopes, while at the same time embodying all her doubts. "I'm not the same girl I was ten years ago."

He didn't so much as blink. "And I'm not the same guy. Congratulations, we've both grown up. You were brave enough to take on the boy. Are you brave enough to take on the man?"

His sharp eyes dared her to respond. Silence was her only option, because there was no good answer.

He stepped closer, trapping her between the tree and his body. A smug little smile tugged at the corner of his lips. "You know you want to. We wouldn't be here if you didn't."

"You haven't changed so much, Shane. You're still a cocky motherf—" His tongue swept the curse off her lips. Another few seconds and he'd stolen her breath. By the time he raised his head, she had one leg wrapped around his hip and both arms clinging to his shoulders. She blinked her eyes open to find the smug smile firmly in place and wondered why her body still responded to it like a hormonal teenager after all this time.

"That's no way to express your forgiveness."

She gritted her teeth and willed herself not to give in to the urge to grind her hips against his. "I didn't say I forgave you."

"You do." His expression went serious. "What's it going

to take to convince you to say it, Sinclair? Need me to say it first? No problem. I—"

"I didn't do a damn thing requiring your forgiveness." A little voice in the back of her mind whispered *except...*into the silence that followed, but she felt sure he wouldn't call her on it. He wouldn't dare

"Did you give me the benefit of the doubt? When you didn't hear from me that summer, did you believe there was a reason I couldn't get in touch, or did you lose faith in me?"

"I...you..." Her ability to construct a counterargument fled in the face of his quiet accusation, and bone-deep panic set in. The only thing more frightening than saying the words he wanted to hear was what might come streaming out of her mouth next. If she relinquished such a crucial stone in the wall of her defenses, would she be able to hold anything back, including feelings she'd banished for years? Feelings she'd have chosen not to have, if emotions worked that way. But here he was, slowly, surely stripping the choice away from her and asking her to trust him while he did it. She fought back the only way she could. She took a step back and shoved him away. "I don't need this."

Big hands caught her shoulders, stopping her retreat. A flex of muscles and she ended up plastered against his chest. "Yeah, you do," he muttered and kissed her. Not hard. Not forceful. He simply brought her mouth to his, moved his lips over hers like he had all the patience in the world, and let her do the rest—as if he knew she would—and, God help her, she did. She drank deep, like a horse led to water.

Need immediately spiked, but her anxiety receded. Volatile as the chemistry was, it nonetheless felt safe. She knew what to do with physical needs—even ones this powerful. She embraced the power. Wanted the urgency. Wanted a driving desire so all-consuming it allowed for nothing else. No examination of feelings, and definitely no conversation beyond the occasional demand, curse, or plea. But when she gathered up a handful of his shirt and tore her mouth from his to pull it over his head, he broke her unstated rules.

"I forgive—"

"Shut up." She reclaimed his mouth and shoved his shirt up his chest. The lure of his bare skin called to her, but she couldn't abandon her post. She made do with her hands, touching every part of him she could reach—smooth shoulders, broad back, the hard planes of his chest, and the enticing little gulley chiseled down the center. She trailed her fingers lower, and his breaths turned fast and harsh in her mouth.

Her head went light from the forced synchronization. Luckily, there was more than one way to render a man speechless. She hooked fingers into the waist of his pants, popped the button, and lowered the zipper. He sprang right into her hand, hot, thick, and heavy. A groan rumbled in his chest, then another as she gripped his shaft and rubbed her palm over his wide, blunt head. A couple circles—not too hard, not too soft, exactly as he'd showed her all those years ago—and she coaxed forth enough fluid to make her palm glide.

She slid her other hand up his length, gripped the base with her lubricated hand, and began long, alternating pulls, adding a little twist at the end just the way he'd always liked.

He still did. His mouth crashed over hers, again and again, the kisses wet and reckless. Whiskers abraded her sensitive lips. Every other sensitive part of her body tingled in response, anxious to experience the same rough treatment.

Switching to a one-handed hold on his cock, she lifted him and cupped his balls. His shudder vibrated through her so deeply it might as well have been her own. No, he wasn't a teenager anymore, but a man could only take so much. She wasn't a teenager, either. She'd picked up a few skills of her own. Another hard pull—he groaned as she administered it—a feather-light brush along the nerve-packed zone behind his balls, and conversation would cease to be an option for him. Victory hovered within reach, so close she could practically taste it.

Which only left her all the more stunned when she suddenly found her arms dragged above her head and pinned there by a big, domineering hand.

Chapter Thirteen

Shane made sure his hold on her wrists was firm, but not bruising. He walked that fine line to convince Sinclair she was well and truly caught—because he couldn't let her touch him again—but he didn't want her scratching the backs of her hands against tree bark in an effort to twist out of his grip. To increase his odds of success, he returned the unrelenting assault she'd made on his mouth and did his level best to kiss her into compliance. Only when her arms went limp and her body rubbed restlessly against his did he lift his head.

Desire and anger warred in her eyes. A combination he couldn't resist. "I'm not going to come in your hands, Sinclair, or your mouth. I'm coming inside you, and you're going to say the words right before you take my cock."

She made a small, negative noise, but he swallowed it and then drowned out her moan with the rasp of the zipper running down the front of her vest. When it hung open, he pushed the padded fabric aside and palmed her breast through her thermal shirt. Whatever she had on underneath strapped her tight and denied him the feel of her soft, giving flesh. Frustrated, he tunneled beneath her shirt, all the way to the thick band of elastic under her breasts. It gave barely at all. He felt around for a clasp and came up empty. Finally, he just shoved it out of his way, manhandling her tits in the process. What might have started as a little cry of shock turned into a grateful sigh when those warm, soft globes sprang free from the unforgiving spandex confines. He soothed them in his hands. "Jesus Christ. How'd you get into that thing?"

"It wasn't easy."

Nothing about tonight would be, apparently, but he'd persevere because she wanted this, too, even if she wished she didn't. As if reading his mind, she arched into his touch and pled, "Don't stop."

"Don't make me stop." He pinched one tight nipple. "Say it."

She shook her head and wriggled her wrists out of his hold. Like a boxer readying for a fight, she shrugged her vest off. "I've never punched anyone before, but you keep this up, and trust *me*" — she broke off to pull her shirt and the torture device of an undergarment over her head — "you'll be the first."

Had he called her stubborn? She was downright ornery. He shed his shirt and then toed his boots off while she watched him with a defiant expression. With more calm than he felt, he got rid of his pants, straightened, and waited while her hot gaze raked his cock like a brutal touch before making its way back to his face. "You're going to say it, baby girl. If I have to take a punch or two in the process, so be it, but you're going to get down on your knees and say it like you mean it. The words are going to ring in your ears as I slide inside you."

Her eyes widened, and her mouth fell open. Satisfied with the game plan, he dropped to *his* knees and turned his attention to getting her naked, first tugging off one shoe, then the other, and then the leggings. His whole body pulsed at the sight of her wearing nothing but lamplight. Memories didn't do her justice. How could they? He leaned in and kissed her just below her navel.

"Is this your twisted idea of a challenge?"

He tipped his head back and looked at her. "It's a promise."

"We both want this. Why complicate things?"

He got to his feet. Well aware he was risking his balls, he replied, "You know why," and kissed her again.

Her groan tasted sweet on his tongue. Fingernails trailed from his shoulders all the way down his back, stopping at his ass to dig in and urge him forward. She rose onto her toes and twined a leg around his thigh. "Dammit, Shane, I didn't ask for any promises—"

"Yes, you did." Sliding an arm around her waist, he pulled her away from the tree. A pivot, a drop he controlled, and he had her on her back on the blanket. He planted a palm next to her head and braced himself on his arm. He used the other arm to hitch her leg over his shoulder. "You gave one, and you accepted one in this very spot." Then he dragged the head of his cock through her center. "Does that stir any memories?"

She gasped. Her hands fisted in the blanket, and her spine bowed until her chin pointed to the sky. "That was a lifetime ago."

"Doesn't matter." He did it again, drawing a lazy figure eight this time, hitting her clit solidly and then circling her entrance while she writhed under him. "There's no statute of limitations on forgiveness."

Her chest heaved as he increased the pressure and pace of the stroke. Her cheeks flushed. She rocked her hips and let out a tortured moan. He sympathized, because making his case hurt him as much as it hurt her. Sweat stung his eyes. His muscles burned from the strain of holding back. And his cock…his cock pounded like a second heart. But he didn't let up. "Why did you follow through on the tours, Sinclair?"

"Because…because we had a deal."

He slowed his stroke and lingered at her threshold, circling, circling. Killing himself. "Try again. I had no way of enforcing the deal, and we both know it. You didn't have to be there. Not even once, but you were. Every time. Why?"

"Fuck it, Shane, I was curious."

"Uh-uh. The night at the wedding was more than enough to satisfy any casual curiosity and put to rest any doubt in your mind that something still sparked between us." Those sparks were a raging fire right now, but he just kept fanning the flames—moving fast as he stroked upward, and slow as he navigated the downward curve. "By the end of the first tour at the high school, you knew beyond a shadow of a doubt I wanted you." He angled up and whipped her clit again. "Why'd you keep coming? Why wade through painful memories to get some truth between us?"

Her head whipped back and forth. "I don't know… closure."

If he wasn't already in such a world of hurt, he would have laughed. Instead he parked the head of his cock right at the tight, wet entrance quivering for a good, hard thrust. He flexed his hips and tested the resistance—and his own sanity. "Does *this* feel like closure?"

"Oh, God." Her eyelids fluttered down. Her heel dug into his back. "No."

"Why are you here with me, right now?" He eased back— had to—before instincts took the decision out of his hands. The retreat earned a sob from Sinclair.

"You know why," she whispered.

Game over, thank Christ. He reared up, pulling her with him until he had her on her knees straddling his lap, his hands under her ass to keep her from jumping the gun. "Tell me. Say it like you mean it."

"I—" Slender arms encircled his head, and her breath hitched. "I forgive you." As soon as the last word passed her lips, he was inside her—*home,* a voice in his mind insisted—and then thought ceased as pleasure so intense it qualified as pain shot through him. From a universe away, he heard her cry his name and fought his way back to her.

"Thank you," he murmured and started moving her on him with some attention and skill, because as unforgettable as their first time had been, he'd just as soon not fuck her like an eighteen-year-old amateur. Deliberately setting the rhythm a little slower than she wanted, he lifted her and brought her down hard enough to force a gasp out of her before he took her up again.

He wanted to kiss her, but she clung to him tightly, her chin digging into his skull with every move, and he wanted that, too, so he settled for pressing his face to the side of her throat. He quickened the rhythm. "I know that wasn't easy for you. I'm going to make you another promise, Sinclair,"

"Don't—"

Her word dissolved into breathless whimpers that meant only one thing. He picked up the pace. Suddenly, she arched up, her body strung so tight she trembled in his arms…and that was it for him. The ground slid away under his feet. He was falling. Fighting it, but falling. He forced once last burst of obedience from his muscles and thrust, rocking her hard.

Through a descending fog of oblivion, he managed to say, "I will never let you down again."

Chapter Fourteen

If walls could talk, Sinclair mused as she pulled up to the curb in front of the Oglethorpe Inn. The last time she'd been here, she'd been resolutely single, attending the Daughters of Magnolia Grove's annual Christmas Eve dinner with her family, watching Beau and Savannah crack apart when Mrs. Pinkerton had congratulated them on the new baby Beau hadn't yet known they were expecting. Little oops. Beau hadn't taken it well, to say the least. He'd let fear left over from a tragedy in his past dictate his reaction.

At the time, she'd been furious on her sister's behalf, and not especially concerned with the reasons behind his ugly accusations or hasty retreat. She understood fear and distrust better now than she had at Christmas — or at least understood she shouldn't hurl stones while standing in the middle of her own house of glass. Fear and distrust had been invisible copilots of her life since the summer when letting her heart take the controls had crash-landed her in a truly awful place. She and Beau actually had a lot in common when it came to coping mechanisms.

But people changed. Beau had. Shane definitely had. Maybe she could, too?

She cut the engine and stepped out onto the sidewalk. Maybe she already was changing? Not bravely, or particularly gracefully, she had to admit, but then again, if someone had told her last Christmas that the very near future would find her on her knees under the willow tree where she'd surrendered her virginity, telling Shane Maguire she forgave him, she would have laughed her ass off. A week after putting her feelings for Shane into words—and accepting the words from him—and nothing disastrous had happened. Fate wasn't using them as chew toys, so far. She'd survived his version of a tour of downtown Magnolia Grove, the highlight of which had involved some very sinful acts in the parking lot behind the Presbyterian Church—yes, they could still do it in a car. He'd survived another Sunday dinner at her parents' house before catching a red-eye to Los Angeles for a client in need. When she'd walked him out, he'd seemed a little tense and unsettled. Mind already on his work, she'd assumed, and then he'd thanked her for dinner and kissed her senseless, and she'd let it go. It wasn't until a day later, when she'd driven downtown and passed the inn that she'd realized he was essentially living like a visitor in his own hometown—hotel, suitcase, rental car, laptop. Other than the view out the window, was it really so different than being in Los Angeles, or Virginia, or wherever?

The thought had left a slippery feeling in her stomach. It was. Of course, it was. He had connections to Magnolia Grove. But maybe it wouldn't hurt to remind him?

When he'd called yesterday to let her know he'd be back in town this afternoon, she'd informed him she'd meet him at his hotel at three p.m. sharp. She was taking charge of their next tour.

Now that the moment had arrived, however, a part of her wished she'd planned their tour for tomorrow, so they could spend this Saturday afternoon making up for six days of separation. Well, several parts of her, actually. She'd missed him. Her phone dinged with an incoming text. She lifted it from the inside pocket of her purse, and checked the screen.

I'm ready for my tour.

Her eyes automatically lifted to scan the three orderly rows of shutter-flanked windows decorating the front of inn above the lobby level. Nothing...nothing...then her eyes stalled and her heart cartwheeled. Top floor, end window. Shane stood there, staring at her, his wide, bare chest filling the window, his torso tapering down to where a white towel hung from his hips, only a hairsbreadth above indecent. Her throat went dry, and one of those parts of her that had missed him badly went very, very wet. But she'd made arrangements, and backing out at the last minute repaid someone's kindness with rudeness. Manners forbade canceling the plans, even for the sake of her...parts.

She tore her eyes away from the mouthwatering view and started typing.

You pervert. Stop flashing people from your hotel window, and get your ass down here.

When she looked up again, he was reading his screen. She was too far away to see his expression, but a quick second later her phone dinged again.

I'm not wearing a stitch, and you're ordering me to the street. Who's the pervert? And what does she have in store for my ass?

Okay, she was definitely the pervert for all the highly depraved ideas polluting her mind. Ideas she'd spell out for him in intimate detail. Later.

*Put some clothes on that ass first. Then get down here,
and you'll find out.*

He braced an arm on the window frame and leaned
forward—no doubt to glare down at her. The pose turned
his torso into a lean, rippled monument of masculine beauty
and slid the towel so low it disappeared from view. Finally,
he lifted his phone and texted her, one-handed. Just thinking
about his nimble thumb left her a little sweaty despite the
mild, partly sunny day.

*Bossy. Sure I can't tempt you upstairs? I'm told it's a
damn fine ass.*

She grinned in spite of herself but shook her head.

*Put something pretty on it. Quickly. My tour starts in
ten minutes, and I don't want to be late.*

After she hit send, she looked up. He was reading the
text. Once he finished, he straightened and gave her a salute.
Then he tossed something aside and turned away from the
glass, deliberately offering her a view of his rangy shoulders,
the long, muscular line of his back, and his stark naked, and
damn fine, ass. She slumped against the side of the Tahoe as it
disappeared from sight.

A few minutes later one side of the elaborately frosted
glass door of the inn swung open. Her heart did more
acrobatics as Shane stepped out. Instead of making her forget
the staggering abundance of hard muscle hidden beneath,
the long-sleeved black polo he wore emphasized the expanse
of his shoulders, the loose-limbed strength of his arms, and
the formidable wall of his chest. A triangle of white T-shirt
peeking out from his collar teased her with the knowledge
two layers of fabric now separated her from his warm, vital
flesh. He'd haphazardly tucked the very front of his shirt into

the waist of his jeans—wash-whitened at the stress points along the button fly and a shade darker just below, where the denim cupped a truly impressive bulge.

Long, powerful thighs flexed as the bulge drew closer. A deep voice drawled in her ear. "You keep looking at your favorite toy like that, baby girl, and it's going to want to come out and play."

She ran her tongue along her suddenly dry lips, and he groaned. "Too late." A big hand closed around the lapel of her jacket and dragged her to him. "It's good to see you," he murmured and then waited a beat for her to say it as well, but her breath deserted her. Before she ruined a perfect moment due to emotional clumsiness, she closed the space between them and kissed him. If he noticed her fumble, he didn't hold it against her, just kissed her back, and kept right on kissing her until she wrapped her arms around his neck and leaned into him so she could have more. More of his lips, his tongue… more of him. When he trailed his mouth over her chin, a moan erupted from deep in her throat. When he nibbled his way along her jaw, the moan turned to a sigh of surrender.

"Let's go upstairs," he whispered around her earlobe.

"My, my. This sure is interesting."

Shane's muffled curse vibrated in her ear, but he lifted his head slowly, unhurried. She opened her eyes and turned to face Ricky Pinkerton. A couple of men she recognized as some of his cohorts…okay…co-investors, walked with him.

"Pinkerton," Shane said with the briefest of nods. "Gentlemen."

"Maguire," Ricky returned. "Sinclair, always a pleasure. I didn't realize you two were so…friendly."

"Surprise," she shot back.

"It is," he replied. "It explains a lot, too."

She heard something snide in Ricky's tone, but Shane answered with a disinterested, "You think?"

"Uh-huh. Now I understand why we're making a mountain out of a molehill over a little creek water."

Shane's eyebrows went up. "Because I'm doing my job?"

"Right. You're Mr. Ethics. No personal interests in play for you."

She opened her mouth to tell Ricky he wouldn't know ethics if they smacked him in the face, but Shane beat her to the reply. "None that conflict with my professional duties, which is more than I can say for some."

Red rushed into Ricky's face. He stepped into Shane's space and puffed his chest. "I live here. I work here. My family is here. So, you bet your ass it's personal for me. I don't need you showing up after all these years and interfering just to convince people you're some kind of big shot. Everybody knows the creek isn't a problem."

"Fine, Pinkerton." Shane stepped up, too, and Ricky immediately retreated a half step. "Don't fortify the creek banks. Roll the dice. See what happens. I'm sure your personal opinion will satisfy the planning commission, and the other investors. They probably don't even care what a certified water resources engineer has to say on the matter."

Silence ruled for a full ten seconds. Then one of the cohorts cleared his throat and mumbled, "Ricky, we're gonna miss our tee time if we don't shake a leg."

"Don't let us hold you up," she said. The closest course was at the country club two towns over and thirty minutes away. "Enjoy your drive. Better not cancel that membership any time soon," she added under her breath as Ricky passed.

"Sinclair, kiss my—"

"Watch it." Shane directed the warning to Ricky and held the Tahoe's driver's side door open for her.

She laughed as she climbed in. Then, just to remind Ricky who really called the shots, she taunted, "Give my regards to your grandma."

The slam of the door didn't quite cover Ricky's response.

"Go on and go, Maguire. You don't belong here. You didn't belong ten years ago when we kicked your ass out, and you don't belong here now."

• • •

Shane sat in Sinclair's passenger seat, watching the scenery pass by without really seeing it. Ricky rubbed him the wrong way just by breathing, but the motherfucker had taken irritation to a whole new level in less than three minutes, simultaneously cockblocking him, insinuating he had personal motives for bringing up the flood risk created by the golf course, and being a prick to Sinclair. If Pinkerton had half a brain in his inflated head, he'd be helping find a solution to the situation instead of pretending no problem existed. Instead, Shane was going back and forth with an architect, a structural engineer, and a contractor about how to retrofit a two-hundred-year-old foundation to raise the barn to an appropriate flood-protection elevation.

"It's good to see you, too," a voice said softly from beside him.

Well, there was that. Irritation faded. He turned and regarded her, taking in her perfect profile and the pretty blush decorating her cheek. He decided to push his luck. "And exactly why is it good to see me, Sinclair?"

"Because of the sex."

He felt a smile tug at the corners of his mouth. Stubborn woman. "I don't buy it. We could be back at the inn, scratching that itch, but you refused my personal invitation. Try again. Why are you happy to see me?"

"Um…" She bit her lip and stared through the windshield. "It might have something to do with the fact that I missed you."

Irritation gone. But now he regretted more than ever that they weren't back at his room, where he could reward her lavishly for volunteering the words he knew scared the crap out of her. He slid his hand over her leg, squeezing her thigh through the baggy jeans she wore. How quickly could he have them undone? Pooled around her ankles? All he needed to do was get her to stop the car.

He leaned in and nuzzled behind her ear. "I missed you, too." He swept his palm up her leg, to her hip, and then fiddled with the tab of her zipper. "Pull over."

Surprisingly, she slowed the car. He'd figured on this requiring more effort on his part, because back at the inn she'd been so dead set on taking the tour she'd arranged. He skimmed his tongue along the rim of her ear. She shivered and applied the brake.

"We're here."

A distinctly cautious tone had crept into her voice. He lifted his head to see how secluded a spot she'd chosen…and froze. The heat licking along his veins fizzled. "Here?"

She nodded. "Yes."

"This place doesn't have anything to do with us."

"Of course, it does, Shane. This place helped shape you." With that, she opened her door and hopped out.

He sat still for another moment, inspecting the small post-war house where he'd grown up, with its sagging porch, faded paint, and cracked asphalt driveway. Ten years hadn't altered much. Someone had planted a raggedy-looking pine tree in the front yard at some point, and the screen door was different, but otherwise, no big changes. Certainly no big improvements.

But apparently, that was about to change. Mayor Campbell's wife, Deanne, came down the drive to greet Sinclair. A realtor by trade, the mayor's other half had leveraged the collective Campbell talents and created a healthy side business buying, remodeling, and flipping underappreciated properties. He opened his door and unfolded himself from the passenger seat.

"Shane, sweetie," she called to him when he started up the drive, "it's good to see you outside of city hall." He took the hand she offered and accepted the encouraging little squeeze she gave him. "When Sinclair called me and said y'all would like to swing by and take a look around, I was surprised at first, but then she reminded me your family lived here."

He nodded. "About twenty years, I think. They moved in when Derek was a baby."

"Well, I can understand you wanting to look the place over before Jim and I whip it into shape. Not much has been done yet." She turned and led the way along the narrow concrete walkway to the front door. "The guys have mostly just hauled junk out. Old Roy Hamilton's family rented it after your parents left, and he spent about eight years here, hoarding away, before he passed on—God rest his soul. Watch yourselves here," she interjected and pointed at the bowing porch steps. "Then it sat empty for a couple years before I finally convinced Ethel Finch to sell it to me because its days as a rental were *O-V-E-R*. So, anyway"—she swung the front door open—"I warn you two, it's a dingy mess in here."

Sinclair took his hand and cast a careful look at him as they followed Deanne inside.

"We're keeping the floors—that's good, solid oak under all the dust and scratches," the older woman chattered. "The kitchen's this way," she went on, like she was showing the house, and then laughed at herself and looked at him before adding, "but, of course, you know the layout."

"It's coming back to me," he replied, still not sure how he felt about being there—or why Sinclair had felt the need to bring them here.

"Well..." Deanna peeked at her watch. "I'd better be on

my way so I'm not late to an open house. I'm going to lock the front door behind me. The kitchen door can be locked from the inside, so if you could exit from there when you're done exploring, and just be sure it's shut tight, I'd really appreciate it."

Sinclair spared him a glance, and a small smile, and then turned to Deanne. "Will do. Thanks, Deanne."

"Oh, no problem, hon. I hope you'll both come back and look around once we've remodeled."

Shane listened with one ear as the ladies exchanged a final round of niceties, while his eyes took in the empty shell of a living room. His mind, however, saw back in time. A door closed, and a second later Sinclair stood beside him.

"This was the living room?"

"Yeah." He sounded like he'd swallowed gravel. He cleared his throat and went on. "There was a long, brown sofa against this wall, and, over there"—he pointed to the right— "an oversize eyesore of a recliner my dad practically lived in. Over here"—he indicated the wall opposite the sofa—"we had the TV on a fancy cabinet my mom was so proud of because she'd won it at a church raffle and swore it was an antique. I'm pretty sure they still have that ugly old thing." He laughed. "If it was an antique, it was wasted on us. Half the time, the living room floor looked as though that cabinet had puked PlayStation components all over it."

"Oh, you were one of the lucky kids," Sinclair said. "Savannah and I begged, but our parents refused to get us a PlayStation. Dad told us it would be too depressing for him to come home and see his girls glued to a screen, blowing up the planet."

"Derek and I worked on our mom for the better part of a year before we talked her into buying it."

"I'm betting she worked you, too."

He inclined his head. "She tried, extracting promises from

us to stop wailing on each other, and keep our rooms clean, and do our chores. We agreed to everything, naturally, and followed through on none of it, but I suspect she knew all along our promises weren't worth the breath it had taken to utter them."

Sinclair's lips curved into a smile. "But she bought it for you anyway."

"Probably to shut us up. We had fun with it, though. Kyle Grieger and Marc Waggoner from down the street would come over, and we'd all play Final Fantasy, or Grand Theft Auto, until Dad would get home and commandeer the TV."

"God, Kyle Grieger. There's a name I haven't heard in eons. Whatever happened to him?"

Shane racked his brain and came up mostly empty. "I don't know. He got busted in Atlanta with Derek—for grand theft auto, ironically—and I lost track after that. Marc was my year. He went to college, met a girl, got married, and now he's an actuary in Philly."

"Ever see him?"

He nodded. "We grab a beer whenever I'm in town."

"That's nice, keeping up a connection from your childhood." She graced him with a cryptic smile and ambled through the archway leading to the kitchen. He followed.

She stood at the kitchen door. "Can you get to the backyard through here?"

"Uh-huh." The warped frame protested when he pulled the door open. The wooden step down to the basic concrete slab of a back porch looked rickety. "Careful," he said and held her elbow while she stepped down. The slat groaned under his weight when he followed, and rotted sections splintered. He gave his next move a moment's consideration and then shifted his weight to one foot and brought the heel of his other foot down hard. The wood cracked.

Sinclair turned around, startled, and gave him a wide-eyed look. "Are you okay?"

"Fine." He stepped down to the concrete, leaned over, and hand-pried the broken halves off the supports. After he stacked them against the wall, he crouched and brushed away leaves and debris that had accumulated under the step. And there they were. Two sets of handprints in the cement. One a little larger than the other, but both small.

Sinclair crouched beside him and used a finger to trace the right hand of the smaller set of handprints, lingering in the valley between the ring finger and little finger. "Are these yours?"

The same valley on his right hand tingled. "Yep."

She placed her palm over the imprint and rested it there. "How old were you?"

"Five or six. The old slab had pulled away from the house, and after my folks complained enough, the landlord sent a crew over to break it up, haul it off, and pour a new one. Dad told us to stay away from the drying cement, but Derek and I didn't want to hear that. The next morning, my dad spotted the handprints and was like, 'What the hell is this?'"

"Busted?"

He laughed. "We gave him our best innocent looks and told him some kids must have come along in the middle of the night. He stuck our hands in the prints and said, 'Yeah, right.'" Another reluctant laughed rumbled up from his chest. "We didn't think it through."

"Well, you were only five. And a pristine, freshly poured expanse of wet concrete is pretty impossible to resist."

He looked over at her. He'd needed this. He couldn't say why, but he had, and the fact that she'd known made him want to get her back to that barn of hers, lay her across the big bed, and give her everything *she* needed. "When I was five. Nowadays there's something else I find impossible to resist."

She took his hand and wove her fingers through his.

"Come on. Show me the rest of the house you grew up in."

He got to his feet and tugged her up. "We're still on the tour?"

"I booked the grand tour, Maguire. I want my money's worth."

"All right. Follow me." He led them inside and down the hall, pausing by the house's only full bath. "Bathroom," he said, though the thing spoke for itself.

"Wow. Four people, one bathroom. That must have been challenging at times."

"My parents had a half bath in their bedroom. Derek and I shared this one. Kind of the way two Rottweilers share a kennel, but we managed."

"Savannah and I shared a bathroom, too. I don't imagine yours looked like an Ulta pop-up shop."

"Not so much. For a long time, the tub was basically an arsenal full of water guns and other weaponry designed to lure us into the bath. Once Derek hit puberty, the clutter migrated over there." He pointed to the small counter surrounding the sink. "Hair product, zit gel, and some righteously foul cologne Derek used that smelled like vanilla wafers laced with Pine-Sol."

Sinclair grimaced. "Strangely, I know exactly which one you're talking about."

"The first time Derek used it, Dad yelled, 'What the *fuck* is that smell?' This was all the way from the living room, mind you. Derek called back, 'That's the smell of me about to get lucky as *fuck*.' The old man said, 'You'll be lucky somebody doesn't hose you down with a power sprayer.'" A reluctant laugh bubbled up from his chest. "One of the few times I agreed with him."

Memories swirling, he continued down the hall. The door to his parents' bedroom hung open on the right, and to the left, his and Derek's room. He gestured Sinclair inside and then stepped in behind her. Even empty, the cramped chamber was smaller than he remembered. Two twin beds, two nightstands, and an upright dresser had pretty much spoken for all the space. Curious, he wandered to the closet and ran his hand along the doorframe. A layer of paint had been applied sometime during the last ten years, but his fingertips felt out the ladder of short, thin indentations running up the frame. Sinclair traced one with her fingernail. "What's this?"

"Derek and I measured ourselves every six months or so, and much to our mom's dismay, marked our progress with a Swiss Army Knife our grandfather had given us."

"How do you know which mark goes with which of you?"

"For most of this, Derek's the higher mark." He swept his hand up and stopped at shoulder level. "About here, I caught up, and then the marks switch."

"That happened with me and Savannah, too. She's still a little bent about not getting her fair share of the height genes."

"Derek was pissed at first, but then he took to insisting he didn't care because he had the bigger dick."

Sinclair raised one dark eyebrow. "I can't speak with certainty, but I find that hard to believe."

He slung his arm around her shoulder and pulled her into him. "I doubt a strict measurement would bear his claim out, but Derek definitely had the bigger mouth."

"That, I believe." She turned into him, resting her hands under shirt, along his abs. The feel of her palms on his skin was all it took to have his dick straining painfully against the rivets of his button fly. Her smile turned challenging. "Did you ever sneak a girl in here?"

"Once or twice."

Her fingers hooked into the waist of his jeans, and she dropped to her knees. His head went light as the rest of the blood in his body flowed directly to his cock, causing it to swell to new dimensions.

"So, I wouldn't be the first one to give you a blowjob here?"

"No, baby girl, 'fraid not."

She undid the first button on his fly, then the next, and looked up at him again. "Who wins that distinction?"

His mind spun for a second, working hard to track the conversation, and then skated back almost fifteen years, to pretty, energetic, and, at the time, far more worldly Shannon Grieger. Kyle's sister. He hadn't thought of her in well over a decade. "I don't kiss and tell."

That earned him an eye roll, but she yanked open the remaining buttons. "I guess I'll have to settle for being the last."

"Holy…shit. And the best," he managed. He hadn't bothered with underwear, and she didn't bother with any civilized decencies, either. She wrestled him out and deep-throated him like a pro. Like she'd spent the last six days hungering for him as much as he'd starved for her. Her warmth engulfed him. She cradled him there for a long, extraordinary moment, letting him pulse in the sweet, soft haven of her mouth, and then, keeping her lips sealed tight, she flicked her tongue along his shaft, moving steadily up, up, up to his tip. When she reached it, she cupped his balls and laved the blunt head, lulling him into a false sense of complacency before spearing the tip of her tongue into the agonizingly sensitive opening.

His body went up in flames. His breath exploded from his chest in a harsh grunt that echoed in the cave of a room. She slowly worked her way down, tugging gently, and then not too gently, on his balls as she went. His legs threatened to buckle. Another second of this and he was going to come on his knees in his childhood bedroom, without even understanding what had compelled her to bring him here. No good. He wanted inside her—inside her body and her mind—and getting there required conversation. He threaded his fingers through her hair and tugged her head back until his cock slid out of her mouth and bobbed heavily in the cool air. Little white lights danced around the fringes of his vision, but he blinked them away and brought her beautiful face into focus.

"Why here?" His voice sounded like a rusty hinge.

Her lips curved into the faintest of smiles. "So, the next time you feel like you don't have roots, you remember two little sets of hand prints on a back porch, and height marks notched in a closet door. The next time Ricky or one of his cohorts calls you an outsider, you remember hours of PlayStation with the neighborhood kids, or three minutes of heaven while some slut who shall not be named went down on you in your boyhood bedroom."

She was doing her best to keep things light, but his heart literally skipped a beat. He knelt until they were face-to-face. "You wanted to show me I have roots here?"

"Something along those lines."

That she'd gone to the trouble left him at a loss for words. He considered his upbringing unimportant at best, and depressing at worst. Either way, it had nothing to do with her, but even so she'd taken these memories, dusted them off, handed them back to him, and told him to look again. This was where he came from, whether or not he appreciated the fact. Then she'd gotten down on her knees to show him *she* appreciated it.

"Thank you," he finally managed. Thinking it was time he thanked her properly, he shoved his hand under the loose waist of her baggy jeans and into her panties A quick inhale greeted his touch.

"Well, I had selfish motives, too," she admitted on a breathless exhale.

"Did you?" He eased a finger insider her, and her eyelids fluttered.

"Uh…huh. You've not only been inside my house, you've been in my childhood home—twice. Seen the embarrassing pictures. Heard the embarrassing stories." She slid her hand into her pants and covered his. "I had to even the score."

He moved his hand beneath hers, stroking her in the process, and then pushed deeper. Her body yielded, accepting two fingers this time. Over her gasp, he asked, "Are we even now?"

"Almost." But then she surprised him by bringing her hand to his cheek and touching her lips to his in a tender kiss. "I wasn't one of those friends who came over to play video games, or one of those girls who climbed through your window, so I never got to see this side of your life before. I wanted to. I wanted you to share the memories with me."

"I'll share anything you want. But to be honest"—he paused and circled his fingers—"I'm more interested in making new memories than revisiting the old ones."

Sweat sheened her upper lip. Her tongue darted out to lick it away, and his cock throbbed at the very new memory of her tongue licking it from base to tip. "Did you ever sneak a girl in here and have sex?"

"You're still hung up on the firsts?" He moved his hand again. Kneading her where she was soft. Stretching her where she was tight.

"I want this memory to be unique," she moaned and rocked her hips. "Missionary?"

"Yes." He pressed her mound with the heel of his hand. Her eyes went blurry. Her hips rocked against him.

"Okay. All right. Cowgirl?"

"Yes."

"Well, Jesus, Shane." She rocked again, finding a steady rhythm now, coating his palm with silky heat. "What *haven't* you done here yet?"

"Is that what you're offering me?"

"Yes." She bit the word out and rocked with abandon.

"Are you going to ride my hand first?"

That stopped her in her tracks. "Do I need to?"

He wanted to laugh, but schooled his expression to give nothing away. "Kinda seems like you want to. Not a problem if you do. I'll make you come again…one way or another."

Those blue eyes went round and a shade wary, but she squared her chin. "First things first, Maguire."

"Fine. Just remember, this was your idea." He eased his hand out of her pants and tugged the buttons open. Then he turned her around and positioned her onto all fours. Next, he dragged her jeans and panties down and took his time arranging them before adjusting her knees a little wider. "Comfy?"

She laughed, sounding a little relieved. "Wow. Big, bad Shane Maguire never managed to talk a girl onto her hands and knees in here before now."

"Oh, I did. You're not going to be on your hands and knees." He leaned over her, deliberately letting his cock settle into the valley bisecting her lush, yielding cheeks, and pushed her upper body down until she folded her forearms on the floor. Then, with his hand across the back of her neck, he lowered her forehead to rest on her wrists. Just as slowly, he straightened, closed his fist around his cock, and dragged it down the divide.

"Oh, God." She stiffened and jerked her head up, trapping his cock mid-journey. "Anal?" She craned her neck and looked at him with wide blue eyes. "Really?" Skittish muscles tightened again, giving him another squeeze.

"If you keep doing that, it's going to be me shooting six days' worth of pent-up longing all over your spectacular ass." And with that threat hanging in the air, he closed his eyes and mentally recited the oath of enlistment, taking that crucial five seconds to get himself under control. "Your suggestion would qualify as a first for me in this room, but no, that wasn't what I had in mind." Just to punish her a little for being such a stickler on this "first" business, he tacked on, "But if you want it to be...?"

"Uh, sure. I can't get enough of that action." She dropped her head back down to her wrists and with manufactured nonchalance that fell far short of the mark said, "Go for it."

Yeah, right. No lube. No prep. Just go for it. Little miss voice-of-experience didn't know what the hell she was talking about. He flexed his hips a millimeter, and when every muscle in her body braced, he worked his cock down those tight cheeks, bypassing the uninitiated territory her pride had offered up without consulting her common sense, and continued to his original destination. She trembled when he slid his head around her soft, slick folds—giving her enough to tease her clit and then pulling back almost all the way to the place she claimed couldn't get enough attention. "You've never had it before, have you?"

"Umm..." She rocked her hips up, back, side to side, keeping up with his roaming cock. "Not in this room, no."

"Not ever."

"Okay, no." Frustration got the better of her. "But I'm dying here. It's been six days for me, too, Shane. Whatever you're going to do, you need to do it."

"I appreciate the option, but..."—he sank into her softness—"you've got your favorite toy, and I've got mine. *This* is what I've been dreaming about for the last six days."

She moaned her gratitude, and her internal muscles quickened around him in a flurry of welcome. He clamped his hands on her hips and started to move in slow, controlled strokes.

"Well, the offer stands, just so you kno...ooh...*oh*," she gasped as he drove deep, letting her have every inch.

"Tell you what, Sinclair, when I take that particular

virginity, I'll do it just as carefully as I took the other. I'll lay you down on a blanket under our tree. I'll use my mouth first, and then my fingers, to get you primed, and ready. Once you're there, I'll sit you on my lap and let you take me in — as much as you can, as slowly as you need to. When you're squirming around, when you can't keep still, can't think beyond finding some relief for yourself, I'll put you on your knees, just like this." He braced an arm by her elbow, skimmed his other hand down to cover her quivering sex, and increased the pace and force of his thrusts. "And give it to you good, just like this." His hand became her backstop. She grinded against it every time he slammed into her. The breathless sounds she made when she was about to come punctuated each slap of their bodies. "I won't stop until you press your face into the blanket and come so hard you cry tears of joy."

She arched up, and her body went stiff an instant before her broken sob assured him he'd gotten her there. That's all it took to send him over. The bedroom, the house, hell, the entire world receded to just one thing — him, moving inside her like lightning and then coming in a long, violent rush so profound he felt like he surrendered everything inside him. Body, and soul.

This was his. Not the town, or the house, but the woman. He loved her. Maybe he'd never really stopped loving her and he'd just allowed himself believe letting her go had been the right thing to do. This time around he wasn't letting go. Nobody, including Ricky Pinkerton, could tell him he didn't belong.

Chapter Fifteen

Sinclair took a sip of wine and glanced around Beau and Savannah's apartment, well aware her sister was giving her the eye from across the table. Hoping to maintain control of the conversation, she pointed to the wall behind Savannah and said, "I love that painting you picked up on your honeymoon." The small watercolor from Bora Bora fit in well with the eclectic mix of art in her sibling's large and uniquely varied collection.

Savannah didn't even bother glancing behind her. She nudged her dinner plate away, rested her elbows on the table, and propped her chin across her linked fingers.

The blown-glass pendant lights suspended overhead showered gold highlights in her blond curls and made her look like a younger version of their mother.

"Well, that about covers all your topics, right? We've talked about how the baby's coming along, how your trade show went, and what you have lined up for the jewelry expo next week in New York. You're up-to-date on Beau's schedule—he's sorry he's missing tonight, by the way—"

"Me, too." Something told her she was about to be really sorry, because Savannah shared more with their mother than looks. She would only be put off for so long. Sinclair had held her sister's curiosity at bay for almost a month, thanks to her ability to dodge phone calls and keep her texts short and baby-focused.

"Now it's my turn. For my topic, I choose you and Shane. You decided to give things a second chance, and it's going well."

"Um…is that a question?"

"Not really. Your face tells me as much."

"What's up with my face?"

Savannah laughed. "Have you seen yourself lately? Nobody glows like you unless they're getting it *good*. I don't care how well the trade show went."

At one point in her life, she'd managed to keep a big secret for a pretty long time. When had she become such an open book? Seeking to stall, she got up and cleared their plates. "I can't discuss this without pie."

Savannah pushed back from the table and stood, smoothing the flannel shirt she'd obviously stolen from Beau over her stomach and unconsciously giving Sinclair a glimpse of baby bump. "I'll supply the pie." She walked to the small, galley-style kitchen. "You supply the details."

"There's really not much to tell," she demurred and put the dishes in the sink, while Savannah cut generous slices from a home-baked Dutch apple pie. She handed one to Sinclair, took one for herself, and led them back to the table.

"Your perma-smile says different." She settled herself in her chair and waited until Sinclair did the same. "Soooo, what's the deal?"

Sinclair raised a forkful of pie to her lips. "We're taking a second chance. So far, so good." There was really nothing else to add, so she took a bite of the warm, lattice-crusted treat.

Savannah's Dutch apple was her favorite.

"He's staying in Magnolia Grove?"

"That's the plan."

"Interesting answer. Why not a simple, 'Yes'?"

The pie turned to dust in her mouth. She wasn't qualifying anything. Was she? "I don't mean it that way." She concentrated on scooping up another bite.

"You trust him?"

The second bite stuck in her throat. She put down her fork and managed to swallow. Just. "Ever since he's been back, he's done nothing but keep his word. He does exactly what he says he's going to do…"

"But?"

She winced. The few bites of pie now sat like bricks in her stomach. "It's not Shane I don't trust. It's fate. We both had the best intentions last time around, but first he couldn't follow through, and then I couldn't."

"Sinclair…" Savannah spoke around a mouthful of pie. "You were teenagers last time around. Neither of you had the kind of control over the direction of your lives you have now, as adults. Do you love him?"

The room suddenly felt small and sweltering. She eased her plate away, because the buttery, cinnamon-y smell of the pie was starting to turn her stomach, and searched for some pat answer that would get her sister to back off. What spilled out instead was, "I do."

She clapped her hands over her mouth, but it was too late. The words rang with truth, and she couldn't take them back even if she wanted to.

"You love him," Savannah repeated. "There now. That wasn't so bad, was it?"

Slowly, she lowered her hands. "Oh, God, I do. Not just old, unresolved parts of my heart, but the whole enchilada, and…what the heck are you doing?"

Savannah turned away, but the move did nothing to hide a very audible sniffle. "Don't mind me. It's the hormones. I tear up at the drop of a hat. I can't help myself. Anyway"—she wiped her eyes and looked at Sinclair—"that's wonderful. I'm happy for you. What did Shane say?"

"Uh…"

"Wait. *Have* you told him you love him?"

"Hell, no."

"Why not?" Frustration had her picking up her fork again and stabbing it toward Sinclair. "You just told me you trust him, and everything's going well—"

"It scares the crap out of me, okay?"

"For heaven's sake, why?"

"It's almost too easy this time around. I keep waiting for fate to lob a grenade and blow us up. Again."

"Wow. Welcome to the Beau Montgomery School of Emotional Risk Aversion. You know what finally got Beau over the dread?"

Under the table, she pressed a hand to her stomach. "What?" She really did need to know, because something was seriously wrong with her if she couldn't even talk about being happy without giving herself indigestion.

"He realized even if it all turned to shit tomorrow, he wouldn't have wanted to miss out on us. Everything we already had, everything we'd already experienced, made all the uncertainty worth the risk."

Was she there? After everything had turned to shit the first time, she'd spent plenty of time wishing she'd never met Shane. Wishing she could remove him like shrapnel from her fractured heart and move on. But she couldn't. She'd gathered up the pieces and put herself back together, but he'd left scars that had never faded. Not fully. Maybe because she'd always secretly hoped they'd get a second chance, or maybe she was just a masochist, but if things went wrong for them now, there wouldn't be a third chance. And that made the stakes feel dizzyingly high. If her heart broke again, would she be able to put it back together? A wave of nausea washed over her, leaving her sweaty and shaking.

"Are you okay?" Savannah stared at her, a frown creasing her brows.

"I don't feel so good."

"You don't look so good."

"I'll be okay." The nausea subsided a little, and she mustered up what she hoped was a smile. "For some reason, the pie turned on me tonight."

"Here, try this"—Savannah got up and returned with a large glass of something cloudy—"it's lemon-ginger water."

She raised the glass and gave the concoction a sniff. The citrusy scent didn't turn her stomach, so she took a sip. Then another.

"I hope you're not coming down with something. Maybe you should skip New York and take it easy for a few days instead?"

Sinclair shook her head. "I can't skip the expo. I've already paid, scheduled appointments, meetings… I'm hand delivering a bunch of orders. I'll be fine. I'm probably just dehydrated. Spent all day setting up my booth, manning it, breaking it down, and didn't drink enough water."

Savannah returned to her seat and laughed. "If I didn't know better, I'd say you were pregnant. That's my cure for morning sickness you're sucking down."

"Ha. Ha. We both know that's not possible." Not without an in vitro specialist involved. But as she took another drink—the darn stuff was actually calming her queasies— she consulted her mental calendar and choked a little on her swallow. She was late, and she was *never* late.

"Yeah, yeah. I know what they told you. But be warned." She pointed to her own belly. "Mother Nature loves surprises."

"I know. She already surprised me once. Based on how that turned out, it would take more than a surprise now. It would take a miracle."

Did she want a miracle? Did Shane? *Does it even matter?* She tossed the question at the expanding balloon in her chest that felt a lot like hope. *If you have somehow managed to conceive, you're virtually guaranteed another ectopic pregnancy.*

She took a more careful sip, ran the math again in her head, and came up with the same answer. Miracle or not, if she didn't get her period by tomorrow, she'd be making a stop at the drugstore on her drive home.

• • •

"Light a fire under the civil engineer, Haggerty. They told you they'd expedite the surveys, and it's been over a month since I requested the report—"

"And expedite means, 'within six weeks,' Shane, which they are. Nonetheless, I followed up earlier today when I got your email. Raj had a family emergency and had to fly home to India. He's due back in a few days and will complete and send the report first thing."

Shane paced the hotel room. "They don't have wifi in India? He can't finalize and transmit a report from there?"

Yes, he was being a hard-ass, and no, it had nothing to do with work timelines. It had to do with his whole fucking life being on hold while he waited for a report. He wanted to tell Sinclair he loved her, but this time around he needed to back the words up with actions. He'd promised to protect her home, and he had a decent plan for doing it, but all his discussions with the structural engineer and the architect were purely hypothetical until he had the water displacement information in the report…and knew what the city planned to do about it.

They could deny the permit, but he wasn't holding his breath. On the other hand, the barn could only be raised so far, and there was no point going to the expense if it didn't sufficiently reduce the risk.

"I think the problem is personal, not technological."

"I don't have a personal problem," Shane replied, automatically on the defensive.

"Not *you*. Raj. He's a tad busy right now with his father's funeral. I guess he could balance his laptop on the casket…"

Fuck. "All right. Fine." He ran a hand through his hair and stared out the window of his hotel room at the magnolias lining the town square. "Sorry for his loss."

"We're sending flowers. Why the panic? I thought you said everything was going smoothly?"

"It is." Tight muscles at the back of his neck ached as he tipped his head toward his left shoulder, and then the right. "I'm not panicked. I'm annoyed. Everything's on track, but the city planning commission is holding off on making a decision about the resort's golf course until they get the report. We've got a meeting tomorrow morning, and I wanted to put something in front of them."

"One more week, tops. Is Pinkerton getting fidgety?"

"No more so than usual." Less so, actually, and that was also a problem. The last couple times he'd seen Ricky, instead of hammering at him for an update, the guy had given him a shit-eating smirk. The little prick was up to something. Shane didn't like it. "Even if he is, he'll just have to jack himself off a little longer. It is what it is. I'll explain the situation at the meeting tomorrow. One more week won't kill him."

"Make sure the same is true of you," Haggerty said drily. "Don't go off on this guy during the meeting if shit goes sideways."

He rubbed the back of his neck. "Credit me with a little self-control."

"I credit you with plenty of self-control, but when you call me ready to tear some engineer a new one when he's still within the timeline, I sense you're wound tight. No surprise. This one's more than just a job to you. You're back on your home turf, and your ego's involved. You know as well as I do, most politicians just want to check the box that shows they did a passable amount of due diligence on stuff like this and then approve whatever garners them the most votes. Piled on that, the same whiny asshole responsible for your inglorious departure ten years ago is on the other side of the table, and he's an even bigger asshole now. You can bet your left nut he's going to try and put you in his crosshairs. So, yeah, I'm cautioning you, because one thing I know about assholes, Maguire, is they're full of shit."

"Acknowledged, but it's a nonissue. In a week, I'll have the report, and the city can make an informed decision. In the meantime, I'm not going to give him the opportunity to take any shots at me."

"As it happens, I have a plan to guarantee he can't take any shots."

Shane turned away from the window and crossed to the desk. "What's your plan?"

"Take you out of his line of fire for a few days."

"How're you going to do that?" But he already knew. Not the specifics, but the general concept. Some client was in need, but for the first time in his career, he wanted to tell Haggerty to send someone else.

"There's an off-season storm gathering steam in the Pacific. If you can believe the weather forecasts—and you can't, half the time, but that's another issue—it's going to hit the islands later this week."

Shane leaned over the desk and tapped his laptop to bring up the latest radar. Then he took another second to squint at the screen. "I don't know. Looks like a big, disorganized swirl right now. I don't see how anyone's extrapolating a path from this."

"You have talents I respect, but predicting the weather isn't one of them. Even if it was, we have a world-class hotel chain entrusting us with their emergency planning, and they've got a brand-new, five-star property on the tip of Kauai bracing for the first real test of their disaster readiness. As the architect of those plans, they want you there. This is where we put skin in the game, Shane. I can't tell them we think the forecasts are bullshit. That's not going to fly."

No, he was. And that had to change. He wanted to build a home, a life, and most importantly, a future with Sinclair. He wanted predictability in his schedule, and he couldn't get it while being the first guy on speed dial whenever a client needed a hand to hold. That wasn't going to work for him anymore. And the Seattle project still loomed in his future. He had to have a conversation with Haggerty…just as soon as he carried this project over the finish line. "I've got the meeting tomorrow. I can't leave until Friday, at the earliest." Sinclair flew out Sunday for New York. If he was right about the weather, he'd be back by the time she returned from her convention.

"That works. I'll let the resort know. Expect a text from Barb with the flight details. As long as the forecast holds, plan on a weekend in Hawaii."

Chapter Sixteen

Sinclair stared at the small pink plus sign for a full sixty seconds. Then she scrambled for the box sitting on the bathroom counter, accidentally knocking it into the sink in her haste to reach it. When finally got her hands on it, she didn't need to bother digging for the instructional insert. The picture on the front of the packaging couldn't be clearer, just in case anything had changed since the last time she'd taken one of these tests. Plus meant pregnant. She glanced back at the result window on the wand. Definitely plus. She shook it — why, she didn't know — and looked again. Still plus.

Holy crap. Miracles did happen. The room spun a little as she got swept up onto a carousel of emotions. A dizzying and completely ludicrous whirl of joy took her first, followed immediately by panic. Would Shane think it was a miracle? Did his version of a second chance include a kid? Now?

Then all the questions careening around her head slammed up against a cold, hard wall of reality. Was this pregnancy even viable? Maybe a fragile little bundle of cells sat lodged in her tube, just like last time. The box and the wand clattered onto the counter as she covered her stomach with her shaking hands.

After a moment, she raised her gaze to come face-to-face with her reflection in the bathroom mirror and saw the vestiges of an overwhelmed sixteen-year-old in her eyes.

"Hey, kiddo. Everything okay?"

She turned to find her father hovering in the doorway and rushed to retrieve the pregnancy test and box from where they sat in plain view by the sink. "Oh my God, Dad." Shoving the wand into the box, she faced him.

"Sorry." The stiffness in his voice told her she hadn't moved fast enough. "I stopped to drop off some mail that came to the house. I, uh, saw your car in the drive. I knocked, and I called out, but when you didn't answer, I got worried, so I came in." His gaze dropped to her hands and then bounced up to her face. "Anything you want to tell me?"

So much for hiding the evidence. *Hey, Dad. I'm knocked up. Again.* It had taken so long to restore their relationship last time. She didn't think she could handle him putting that wall of anger and disappointment between them again. A salty burn stung her eyes at the thought, but she shrugged and tried for levity. "Um…no?"

One corner of his mouth lifted a notch. "Oh, come on, kiddo. Let's both try to do better this time around. Start by confiding in me, all right?" He leaned against the doorframe, a Land's End–catalogue shot of casual, no-pressure Dad in his untucked chambray shirt and khakis—but the little smile disappeared. "I know I let you down before, and I'm probably not the first person you'd choose to open up to now, but I'm here. And I love you."

The burning eyes came back with a vengeance. "I love you, too, Daddy." She put the test kit on the counter and walked over to hug her father. Her throat tightened when his arms enfolded her and pulled her close. With her face buried in his shirt, inhaling the reassuringly familiar scents of dryer sheets and Zest soap, she said, "You didn't let *me* down. You've got it turned around, actually. I let *you* down." A painfully hard sob accompanied the admission, followed by scorching tears.

He drew back and gave her shoulders a squeeze. "How about this? Let's go downstairs, have some coffee—er, scratch that—some orange juice, and get things straight."

She let him guide her downstairs while she swiped at her watering eyes and running nose. *Stop crying, for Christ's sake. No matter what nickname your dad calls you, you're not a kid anymore. Dredge up some dignity.* Sound advice, but her tear ducts disagreed.

Her dad deposited her in a kitchen chair. She used the sleeve of her oversize black sweater to wipe her face while he puttered around her kitchen—finding glasses, digging in the fridge, pouring OJ. He placed one in front of her and then sat down in the adjacent chair with his own glass.

She took an unsteady breath and then sobbed out, "I'm s-sorry."

"That's my line. You've never let me down, Sinclair. Never. And I'm sorry if I've made you feel like you did. Ten years ago, you needed support, and understanding, but I was so determined to do what I thought was my duty—and would assuage my anger at some unknown boy who I felt deserved to suffer some consequences—I put us at odds. I yelled at you, and threatened you, and instead of getting the information I demanded, all I managed to do was push you away when you needed me most. What I should have told you a while ago is, in retrospect, I admired your strength for not caving in and giving me the scapegoat I wanted. Then again, I've always been in awe of your strength."

"Well, you know"—she sniffed loudly and hiccupped over another sob—"nothing shakes my steely resolve."

Her father's chuckle told him the incongruence of the

moment wasn't lost on him. "You can handle anything life throws your way. I know this, because I've seen you do it. You might think Savannah is more like your mother, but when it comes to steely resolve and utter fearlessness, trust me, Sinclair, *you* are your mother's daughter. Take that as a compliment, because I mean it as one." He drew in a deep breath before continuing. "You want me to call her? I won't take offense if she's the one you prefer to talk to about the rest of it."

He wouldn't take offense, but he would never be sure he'd said the right thing. And he had. She'd needed a reminder that she'd handled a lot worse, with a lot less life experience behind her. "No." The pressure of fresh sobs building in her chest subsided. Her tears slowed. "No. Actually Dad, you're exactly who I need." She wiped her face and then looked him in the eye, so hopefully he'd know she meant that.

He put down his OJ and rested his forearms on his knees. "So…you're pregnant?"

"Preliminary results say so."

"I didn't think that could happen, without, you know… some science and whatnot."

"Me, neither."

"Shane?"

She nodded, because she didn't quite trust herself to speak.

"History repeating itself, huh?" he asked softly.

"Mom told you?"

"No. I figured it out on my own. The first time he came over to the house for dinner, the lightbulb went off."

She rushed to explain. "He never knew…before. I don't want you to judge him. I didn't tell him until just recently."

"I got that, too. Nobody's that good an actor. He didn't have a clue. Don't worry, Sinclair. I'm not going to reach for my shotgun over something that happened a decade ago.

Let's focus on what's happening now. When are you going to tell him the results are positive?"

She let her gaze drop to the table and traced the worn edge with her fingertip. "I don't know. I thought I would confirm things with the doctor first. Even if I am pregnant, it might not be…um…sustainable."

Her dad stilled her restless hand with his. "He doesn't know?"

"Uh-uh."

He nudged his chair back from the table and aimed a stern gaze at her. "He's not an eighteen-year-old kid this time around, Sinclair. He doesn't need protecting, and he deserves to know what's happening. You both have a stake in this, no matter how it plays out."

"You're right." She rubbed her chest, where an ache centered. "You're right. I need to tell him."

"You do." Her father stood, and she followed suit. "After you talk, if you need me to get my shotgun…" He walked to the door.

"Dad," she hugged him hard—extra hard, for courage— and then stepped away. "You don't even own a shotgun."

He opened the door and stepped out before turning to face her again. Sunlight danced in his eyes, and something else. "Beau didn't know that. Shane doesn't have to know, either."

She smiled, despite everything, and hugged him again. "Give one of those to Mom."

"Will do, kiddo." He leaned down and kissed her cheek. And then he was gone.

No sooner had she shut the door than her stomach suddenly clenched. OJ. Not good. She ran to the kitchen sink to rid her system of eight ounces of Florida's finest, and then washed out her mouth with several handfuls of cold water. Afterward, she drenched a dishtowel, draped it across her forehead, and slumped in a chair at the kitchen table.

Oh, God. Her whole body begged to go back upstairs, crawl into bed, and pull the covers over her head. She really couldn't do this. Not again.

Enough. A firm voice in her head spoke up. *That weak-assed crap has to stop. You're a grown woman. You are strong, and you don't really have a choice. Maybe you didn't see this detour coming, but you're on it. Break the journey down into steps and take the fucking walk.*

Step one. Breath.

She did. Slow and deep, until her pulse settled.

Step two. Call the gynecologist and make an appointment.

Right. She got up and tossed the towel into the sink. Her phone peeked out from the mouth of the purse she'd dumped on the kitchen counter on her way earlier. It felt like a lifetime ago. While she waited for the receptionist to pick up—and immediately ask her to hold—she kept her hands busy riffling through the two days' worth of mail she'd left beside her purse. A FedEx letter caught her attention. She pulled it from the pile, frowning as she noted the return address. What in the world was her landlord sending?

The receptionist came on the line. She concentrated on scheduling an appointment, relieved the doctor could squeeze her in tomorrow morning for a blood test. After she hung up, she held her phone uncertainly. Should she call Shane? Maybe she'd catch him during a break from his meeting?

No. With all due respect to her father, she didn't know anything yet—nothing to justify hijacking his world in the middle of a busy morning.

Welcome to step three. Wait.

Waiting sucked. She tossed her phone into the purse and turned her attention to the mail again—anything for a distraction—and picked up the FedEx envelope. A pull of the ripcord, a tip of her hand, and a fat envelope embossed with the Pinkerton Family Trust return address fell out.

A bad feeling squeezed her stomach, more nerves than nausea this time. She tore the envelope open and unfolded a typed letter backed by…a copy of her land lease, with a red flag stuck to one of the pages. Weird. Had they missed a signature two years ago when they'd completed the paperwork? She skimmed the cover letter.

For violation of paragraph 10(b) of the Lease, pursuant paragraph 21 thereof, Lessor hereby furnishes Lessee with thirty (30) days' notice to vacate the Property.

What the *fuck*?

She read the letter from the beginning, taking in every word this time, and then riffled through the copy of the lease to read the flagged provision. Was this a joke? She flipped to the letter again and looked at the signature at the bottom of the notice—Richard M. Pinkerton.

The snake. She grabbed her purse and stormed out the door.

• • •

"Thanks for the update, Shane. I know I speak for the entire council when I say we appreciate the skill and resources you've brought to this project." Mayor Campbell closed the folder in front of him and smiled across the round meeting table at the other members of the council. "I feel safer already." Then his attention shifted to the wall clock. "Does anyone else have anything to add before we conclude?"

A collective sound of contentment hummed through the room, cut through by the voice he least wanted to hear. "Just one question for Shane."

He turned to Ricky, who'd been fucking around on his phone the entire meeting. "Fire away."

"Any word from the water guy? The one holding up the

golf course permit?"

Had he not paid attention, or was he just being a douche? Shane took a deep breath before responding. "As I mentioned earlier, I expect it next week at the—"

"Yeah, yeah, next week. Maybe that's the best timeline you can swing, but I did a little better." With that, Ricky stood and started sliding documents across the table to each of the council members. "I contacted an expert, and they were able to give an opinion sooner rather than later." He tossed a copy to Shane. "Feel free to read it at your leisure, but, in a nutshell, it says there's no problem. You can review the summary paragraph at the end, if you want more detail. Given the expert opinion, I think we can all agree there's no reason not to put the matter into the planning commission's hands to make a decision on the permit."

"Oh, hey. That's great news," one of the other members said and tucked the report into his attaché. A couple other council members murmured their agreement. A few of them rose from the table, clearly considering the matter settled and the meeting over.

Invisible boxes were being checked all around him.

Shane grabbed the report. "Hold on." He scanned the page and started talking, before he lost them completely. "What expert, Pinkerton? I've never heard of this firm. Nobody on this letterhead appears credentialed as a certified water resources engineer." He flipped the page and reviewed the summary. "All this says is, 'based on the average rainfall over the last twenty years, the proposed bilateral bank build-ups should adequately protect the golf course from seasonal fluctuations in water levels with 'no negative impact to the aesthetics or integrity of the course or surrounding land.'" He looked up and aimed the next question squarely at Ricky. "Where does it address downstream flood risk?"

Four other heads swiveled toward Ricky.

Pinkerton stood. His chin jutted as he pointed to the report. "It says very clearly, no negative impact to the surrounding land. Seems clear enough to me."

"What's the surrounding land? The resort? The parking area? Show me where they define that." He tossed the report on the table like the piece of crap it was. "This doesn't address the specific question of downstream impacts. I can't even tell if they considered anything beyond the perimeter of the property."

"Look, Maguire, you wanted a report from a civil engineer, I got one, and now you're insisting it's not good enough. You know what I think?"

"Gentlemen," Mayor Campbell interjected, but Ricky didn't pause.

"I think you wanted a report from your firm's best buddies, so you could get the findings *you* were looking for, because you've got an old grudge against me. Or maybe because your girlfriend has a problem with people making legitimate use of their land? You should run along and talk to her, because turns out she's the pot calling the kettle black on that score."

Shane felt heat crawl up his neck, but he refused to take any bait Ricky dangled. He folded his arms to keep from clenching his fists. "This has nothing to do with what I want. The city *needs* a thorough report from a qualified expert."

"*Your* expert," Ricky shot back.

"Gentlemen," Campbell said again, with more force this time. When he was certain he had everyone's attention, he went on. "Ricky, submit your report to the planning commission, not the city council. The commissioners are perfectly capable of weighing the information and determining whether it answers the outstanding questions. Shane," he continued and held up a hand for silence when Shane would have spoken, "if your firm's expert has any additional data or opinions to provide, get that report in before their next meeting."

"That's the plan."

Campbell inclined his head. "Good to know. Now," he addressed the entire room, "if there's nothing else, I'm going to wrap this meeting up. I've got another commitment."

The other members of the council nodded their agreement. "Excellent," Campbell said. "Y'all know how to reach me if something comes up." With that, he headed to the door. Ricky shot a smirk Shane's way and then hustled out as well, hot on the mayor's heels.

Mother*fucker*. Shane took his time gathering his things, and letting his temper cool. None of this came as a shock. He'd known going in that Ricky looked a little too self-satisfied not to have some surprise attack arranged. He just hadn't known what form the undercut would take. Now he knew—although the comment about Sinclair being the pot calling the kettle black didn't make much sense, but he wrote it off as another cheap shot to suggest personal bias motivated his reaction to the so-called report. Bottom line? He needed to get their expert's report submitted before the planning commission's meeting next week, which was already the goal, so other than his blood pressure, essentially nothing had changed as a result of Ricky's stunt.

He was no worse off than before the meeting. In fact, he was arguably better off, he decided as he strode out of the meeting room toward the exit, because Ricky had tipped his hand. The arrogant prick hadn't been able to resist showboating at the meeting and shoving his report in Shane's face, but Shane suspected he'd gotten in enough comments to effectively cast doubt on the reliability of the report. On top of that, he could review the copy Ricky had so graciously provided more closely now and submit his questions and concerns to the planning commission—like any good consultant in his position would do. And hey, if it also bought him more time to figure out a solution for Sinclair while the committee reviewed two reports, plus a set of comments, so be it.

Checkmate, Pinkerton. He pushed through the heavy wooden doors of city hall and reached for his phone to call Sinclair. Hopefully she was back from Atlanta. Maybe he could take her to lunch, and—

Commotion at the end of the walkway drew his eye a second after a very familiar, very furious voice reached his ears.

"You are a morally bankrupt bastard."

Sinclair stood at the end of the walkway, practically vibrating with anger, pointing a finger at Ricky. People walking by slowed or stopped altogether to watch the fireworks. Ricky turned a guilty shade of red but strode right up to her until they stood toe-to-toe. "I'm within my rights, Sinclair. You're the one who violated the terms of the lease—"

"This?" She held a flagged page up to his face. "'Lessee agrees not to use the property for any purpose not authorized under local zoning laws?' That's nothing but a convenient legal loophole you're exploiting. When the trust entered into the land lease, you knew I planned to live in the barn. You know I've been living there for two years. I'm a private citizen. You, Ricky Pinkerton, are a city councilmember as well as a stakeholder in the Pinkerton Family Trust. And between the two of us, which one was in a better position to know my portion of *your* land wasn't expressly zoned for residential use?"

"What you didn't know isn't my problem. You've violated the lease. We're terminating it. You've got thirty days to get off the property."

Shane walked faster, not missing the way Ricky pushed out his chest and balled his fists. Sinclair read none of those signals, or if she did, her own temper superseded caution.

"I'm going to make it your problem, Ricky, because this

looks like fraud to me. You entered into an agreement you knew was invalid thanks to the zoning laws—and happily took my money for two years—or you were too stupid to research the rights associated with your own land. Which is it?"

"You've always been a self-righteous bitch, haven't you?" The question came accompanied by a two-handed shove to Sinclair's shoulders. "Haven't you," he repeated and shoved her again, this time hard enough to knock her back a couple steps.

That's where things got blurry for Shane.

A long-buried, liberating current of electricity shot through him, energizing his body and unstrapping it from the constraint of his conscience. He remembered dropping his computer bag. He remembered closing in on them. He even remembered Sinclair turning to him, seemingly in slow motion, all wide-eyed and suddenly pale. The next thing he knew, his right hand throbbed with an undeniably satisfying ache, Ricky lay in a fetal position on the ground, and he was standing over him, saying, "I thought I made this crystal clear ten years ago, you worthless piece of shit. You don't touch her. Not then. Not now. Not ever."

"You broke my nose!"

Probably true, given the amount of blood flowing through the fingers Ricky clamped to his face, but at the moment, it was hard to muster up any regret. "Damn right I did. You touch her again, I'll break it again."

"You're washed up, Maguire." Ricky struggled to his feet and took the handkerchief offered by the middle-aged man standing next to him, who Shane recognized as one of the local attorneys. "Ten years, and you're still nothing but an out-of-control, redneck thug. I'll—"

"You pushed the lady first," a gray-haired bystander chimed in. "If I was twenty years younger, I'd 'a slugged you myself."

A murmur of agreement rippled through the small crowd around them.

"Come on, Richard." The attorney took Ricky's arm. "You have nothing more to say."

An older woman stepped up and wagged her finger at Ricky. "Ricky Pinkerton, you ought to be ashamed of yourself. I'm telling your grandma about this. You can bet your spoiled butt *she'll* have something to say."

Ricky brushed the attorney away and pointed at Shane. "I'll see that the city cancels your contract." With that threat hanging in the air, he took a step away. Then another. Apparently, distance made him bold, because he added, "You're out of here. You got that?"

Shane stood his ground while the lawyer led Ricky away, but with adrenaline subsiding, all the realities set in. He'd fucked up. Lost his shit. Done exactly what Haggerty had told him not to do. Worse, the potential solution he'd come up with for Sinclair had just slipped away like sand through his fist. Mitigating the flood risk by elevating the barn did her no good if she couldn't live there. That hadn't even been part of the equation. He'd told her to trust him, promised he'd figure something out, and he hadn't. He pinched the bridge of his nose, where a headache hammered.

A hand landed on his arm. "Shane?"

Sinclair. He looked up. Looked at her. "Are you all right?"

Her blue eyes lit with fire. "I'm fine. I'm also perfectly capable of handling Ricky myself. You shouldn't have—"

"Don't." He stepped away, because suddenly the air itself felt too close. Technically she might be right, but she was also fundamentally, bone-deep wrong. "Don't even think about telling me I should stand by and let some bully push you around. I've never been that guy, and you know it. If that's what you expect, baby girl, you've got the wrong man."

Jesus, now he sounded like an asshole. The red flags

unfurling across Sinclair's cheeks told him she agreed. He was blowing this on all fronts. Nothing good would come of continuing the conversation at this point. He wasn't going to apologize for what he'd done, nor was he in the mood to get punched by the woman he loved right there on the sidewalk where he'd just flattened Ricky, so he turned and headed across the street to the alley where he'd parked his car.

"Shane!" she called after him. He kept walking. If he wanted to be told he'd fucked up, there were other people he could hear it from who had more immediate standing to say as much. Haggerty, for one. He had to call the man, explain the clusterfuck he'd just caused, and probably accept an immediate and permanent reassignment to another project—if he was lucky.

Though it was only sixty degrees outside, the inside of the Rover felt like a sweatbox. He started the engine and lowered the windows a couple inches before activating Bluetooth and calling his boss. Barb, Haggerty's assistant, picked up on the first ring, and her voice flowed over the speakers. She asked him to hold for a moment. No problem. He had all the time in the world. He dragged off his suit jacket and tie while he waited.

"Solve a mystery for me," Haggerty said by way of a greeting. "Why is Barb waving a note in my face telling me Mayor Campbell is on the other line?"

He winced and summarized everything as briefly as possible.

"That explains it," Haggerty said when Shane finished.

"Sorry," Shane managed.

"No, you're not."

"I'm sorry if this costs the firm the contract," he clarified.

"I'm going to get on the other line and make sure that doesn't happen."

"I can talk to Campbell. This is my mess. Let me clean it

up."

"Cleaning up messes like this is why my name is on your paycheck. It's my primary skillset. *Your* primary skillset is making sure clients are adequately prepared for every plausible threat. We're going to play to our primary skillsets."

Somehow, he got the words, "All right," out through clenched teeth. He'd explain things to Sinclair.

"The good news for you, Maguire, is you're wheels up, just how you like it. Barb's booking you on the red-eye to Kauai as we speak. After that, go straight on to Seattle, as we originally planned for you to do when you finished things in Magnolia Grove."

His plan? What a joke. He felt like a rudderless boat being swept away by rogue currents. Those currents were pulling him off the course he wanted to take, and there was very little he could do about it if he wanted to stay afloat. The situation couldn't get any more fucked up. "Fine."

"Look, shit happens, Maguire. I know you were conflicted about this job from the start. You didn't have much interest in going back home, and maybe you were right. It's not the place for you. Look on the bright side. Magnolia Grove is officially in your rearview mirror. You never have to set foot in that town again."

Shane caught movement in the corner of his eye a second before an icy voice said, "Son of a *bitch…*"

He turned in time to see Sinclair whirl away from the passenger side window. *Wrong again, Maguire. The situation just got more fucked up.*

Chapter Seventeen

"Son of a *bitch*…" She couldn't even finish the sentence. Too many words fought to get out at once, and they choked her. Somehow, despite blinding anger and a hemorrhaging heart, she managed to turn on her heel and start walking. Anywhere. Away.

Behind her, the Rover door slammed. "Sinclair."

"No." She didn't turn around, didn't slow her pace. If she stopped, she just might shatter to a million pieces right there in the stupid parking corridor between the post office and the dry cleaner. Sunlight slanted across the mouth of the alley, highlighting her escape. All she needed to do was get there.

"Sinclair." A big hand closed around her arm. A flex of muscles made momentum her enemy and swung her around to face Shane. "Don't walk away."

"Why? Because that's your move?" She took a step back, but he didn't let go.

"Because I want to explain. I know how everything you just heard sounded—"

"Do you?" Her heartbeat pounded in her ears. "Explain

this, Shane. Did you want to come back to Magnolia Grove?"

Something guilty flashed in his eyes, and she had her answer before he opened his mouth. "No," he admitted.

Her blood heated to a boil. "That night we danced at my sister's wedding, did you have any plan on staying?"

"No. Not then, but—"

"But you lied." Pain sliced through her chest, and she tried to tug her arm free again. "You lied about a lot of things, didn't you?"

"No." He released her arm and ran a hand through his hair. "Look, it's true I didn't originally come back with any plans to stay. I expected to do the job and move on. But then I saw you again, spent time with you, and my plans changed."

"Not from what I heard, they didn't."

He stared at the ground for a moment, expelled a breath, and then looked up at her. "I wanted to get this project across the finish line before discussing my change of plans with Haggerty." His attention shifted to the alley wall, as if the century-old assemblage of bricks and mortar was the most fascinating thing in the world. "It's a tricky situation."

A sound somewhere between a laugh and a sob clawed its way out of her throat. "A tricky situation? You want to know about a tricky situation? Try mine. I'm thirty days from losing my home, I might be pregnant, and the man I was stupid enough to hand my heart to—again—is about to leave town. Again."

Dammit. She hadn't meant to blurt that out. Shane's expression froze.

"What?" He took a step toward her.

She took a step back. "I'm…about to lose my home."

"Not that part."

Those green eyes were too intense. It was her turn to stare at the ground. "I might be pregnant. I took a drugstore test, and it read positive. I have a doctor's appointment tomorrow morning to get something more official."

Hands cupped her shoulders. She looked up to find concern written all over his face—in the set of his brow and the grooves bracketing his mouth. "I thought that couldn't happen?"

There wasn't an ounce of doubt in the question, or suspicion. Gentle as his words were, she couldn't handle them. She spun away and wrapped her arms around her waist to try and hold herself together. "It wasn't supposed to. The test I took this morning could be wrong. But even if it's not, I don't know if the pregnancy will be different than before."

Dammit. She was very far down a road she didn't want to be on. Chances were good she knew exactly where it ended—with Shane, the pregnancy, everything—and the bottom line was, she had no one to blame but herself for winding up here again. Apparently, she never learned.

"We'll figure it out." The low assurance came from close behind her, and then his hands settled on her shoulders again. The urge to lean against him and let herself be supported by his big, sturdy frame nearly overwhelmed her. She dug deep for the strength her father seemed to think she possessed and stepped away. It took another moment, and a deep breath, before she could turn and face him. "There's no 'we.' You're leaving."

A muscle clenched in his jaw. "I'll be back."

"After Hawaii? Or Seattle? Or another ten years? Excuse me if I don't promise to wait this time."

"It's nothing like last time. I have to go, but—"

"Just like last time."

"No. Trust me."

"Trust? Seriously? Look where trusting you has gotten me."

"That's not fair. I didn't know Ricky—"

"Ricky? You think this is about *Ricky*?" Her shoulders

sagged. "Life's not fair, Shane. I learned that lesson ten years ago."

He was in motion before she could blink, closing the distance between them, and holding her in her spot with the sheer determination in his eyes. "I'll be back. And when I get back, I'm going to fix this—all of it—whether you trust me or not."

. . .

"I got good news, and bad news, Maguire. Which do you want first?"

Shane squeezed through a group of Japanese tourists at Lihue Airport to get a better look at the departing flights timetable. "I thought I had the good news. Least that's what I'd call overseeing the execution of emergency plans that helped a key client's new resort weather a tropical storm without a single major issue."

"I call that business as usual," Haggerty responded. "I expected nothing less."

Shane stifled a curse. The board showed a two-hour delay in the departure time for his flight to Seattle. "Fine. I'll take the good news."

"The good news is Magnolia Grove wants the firm to finish the project. They're happy with the plans you drafted, and they're not interested in changing horses this far into the race."

"That is good news. I'll switch my ticket from Seattle to Norcross and be in Magnolia Grove by this evening." He already knew how Haggerty would respond, but some masochistic part of him needed to hear it.

"Not so fast, hotshot. The city council respects your skills, but they think things might go smoother if someone else comes down to deal with the face-to-face interactions."

Peel the spin off that statement and it meant, essentially, he'd been fired as the director of the project. The knowledge left a bad taste in his mouth. Even though he'd expected the outcome, it hurt. A lot. Twice now, he'd been booted from his hometown in the name of keeping the peace. Deep down, he'd harbored hope things would go his way, this time. But history did, indeed, repeat itself.

You really are washed up there. He swallowed that bitter pill and then, what the hell, decided he might as well find out which hungry young project manager had benefitted from his fuckup. "Who are you sending?"

"I'm going. This one's not delegable."

"Awesome. I've got the boss as my own personal janitor. I hope this concludes the bad news portion of this call."

"Get real, Maguire. I haven't gotten to the bad news yet."

Well, shit. Was it worse than spending the last three days reaching out to Sinclair via text and voicemail, and getting no response? Worse than the text he'd finally received from her in the wee hours of the morning, his time, stating simply, "I'm pregnant," which answered one question but left an assload of others unaddressed. Could the doctor determine viability? He figured they could, at least for now, because otherwise she would have sent a different text. Something like, "Adios, motherfucker. Thanks for nothing." So yeah, they were on track to be parents. Was she excited? Scared? Was she okay? He had no fucking idea because she was stonewalling him.

And he was making it easy for her, because the whole goddamn universe was conspiring to pull him away. "What's the bad news?"

"Despite getting soundly convicted in the court of public opinion for bullying Miss Smith, and basically asking for the beatdown you dished out, Pinkerton's still got some clout around town. He convinced the planning commission to fast-track the golf course approval based on the plan and report he submitted."

His heart sank into his boots. "They approved it?"

"Less than twenty-four hours after you left."

Perfect. The one thing he thought he could count as an accomplishment evaporated like mist. Failure landed on him like the proverbial ton of bricks—one heavy blow at a time. Successfully completing the project? Fail. Proving to his hometown a Maguire boy could make something of himself? Fail. Protecting Sinclair's home? Fail. Winning back the woman he loved? That was shaping up as the most spectacular fail of them all.

"From what I learned this morning," Haggerty continued, unaware he'd thrown Shane into a tailspin, "Pinkerton and his cronies wasted no time getting a crew up there to start building up the banks."

Shit. Shit. Shit. Apparently, he said one—or three—of those shits out loud, because Haggerty made a sound of agreement. "Not our shit, at least, because our fingerprints aren't on Pinkerton's report. When ours comes in later this week, I'm confident it's going to reflect everything you spelled out for them. Of course, by then they'll have seen for themselves."

"What do you mean?"

"April in Georgia, son. How long do you think it will be before they get a soaker?"

He did a search on his tablet. About twelve hours, according to the latest weather reports. Being right offered little comfort if it came at the expense of Sinclair's home. As if he weren't feeling impotent enough, fate tossed one more thing out there over which he had absolutely no control and made a mockery of his big talk about fixing everything. By the time Sinclair got home from New York, the barn would be flooded, and there wasn't a damn thing he could do about it.

Or was there? He stared down the crowded terminal, to

where TSA had stacked a low wall of checked luggage waiting to go through a security screening. He blinked and pulled his vision into focus. Ideas clicked into place in his mind and energized his tired system. *Fuck that. You told her you'd fix this. Fix it.*

"Change of plans, Haggerty. I can't go to Seattle yet."

He scanned the departing flights board and started calculating. He had calls to make, planes to catch. Over the line, his boss sounded surprisingly calm.

"You don't say?"

"Personal emergency."

"I wondered when this was coming. All right. Do what you gotta do. Truth is, the client isn't expecting you until next week anyway."

The information put a pause in Shane's planning. "How'd you know I was going to need personal time?"

"I remember the one that got away. I didn't figure you for the type to let her slip through your fingers twice. Go get her, Maguire."

"Thank you, sir."

"Then get your ass to Seattle. After Seattle, we'll discuss training some of the project managers to take on more client-facing legwork, but in the meantime, our contract flies you home every weekend. I trust this time you'll be wanting to take advantage of that perk?"

Shane grabbed his bag and shouldered his way to the ticket line. "That's the plan."

Chapter Eighteen

"Where are you?"

Sinclair adjusted the earpiece of her cell-phone headset. "My flight just landed. I'm at the airport." She unlocked a luggage cart from the kiosk while on the other end of the line her sister relayed information to someone—presumably her husband.

"Beau says the roads are ugly thanks to this rain we're having. Want to come over for dinner and spend the night? We finished setting up the second bedroom."

Second bedroom, aka "nursery," Sinclair thought and wondered if she'd be needing one of those in about nine months…and if so, where the hell she was going to put it? "Thanks, but no. I've got to get home." While she still had one. She appreciated her sister's offer. Savannah had been nothing but supportive since Sinclair had called her Thursday after her confrontation with Shane and dumped the disaster of her life all over her poor sister. She'd cried long-distance tears of joy when Sinclair had phoned from the middle of a Manhattan jewelry show yesterday morning to relay the news she'd received from her gynecologist — the pregnancy test was positive, and initial hormone levels suggested the baby was exactly where it should be.

"How are you feeling?"

Elated, sick, terrified, sick, hopeful, sick. "Fine." She snagged the first of her two checked bags and loaded it on the cart.

"Have you talked to Shane yet?"

"No." Savannah already knew she'd opted to inform Shane of the test result via text, and had made no secret of the fact she disagreed with that decision.

"He didn't respond at all? Not a word?"

"He texted." She grabbed her other bag from the carousel, stacked it on the cart, and wheeled toward the exit.

"Are you really going to make me ask?"

"Savannah, I'm standing in the middle of an airport, here."

"I don't care if you're standing in the middle of the Vatican. What did he say?"

She sighed and pulled her cart to the side, accidentally cutting off a businessman in the process. He glared as he drew even with her. "You want to know what he said when he found out I was pregnant?" The businessman's expression froze, and he hurried past as if she might throw a net over him. Men.

"Spill it."

"This won't take long. It was only two words."

"Sinclair…"

"Okay. Okay." She took a deep breath. For some stupid reason, her heart skipped a beat at the idea of saying the words out loud. "He texted, 'Trust me.'"

Silence followed. Finally, she asked, "Did you hear me?"

Then she heard it. A sniffle.

"Don't even."

"I c-can't help it," her sister replied and sniffed again. "You'll see. Anyway, as two-word replies go, that's a pretty good one. Can you do it?"

"Trust him? I don't know. He lied to me. I know that doesn't necessarily sound like a big deal, given everything at stake now, but it is to me. How do I know he didn't lie about everything?"

"Because you *know*," her sister insisted quietly. "You knew how he felt about you ten years ago, and you know how he feels now. And underneath the completely understandable anger you're experiencing, you know how you feel, too. For that reason alone, you need to give him the chance to explain."

She closed her eyes and let the truth of her sister's words sink in—the near inevitability of them. She'd loved Shane Maguire for ten years. He'd been her first. He'd be her last. It would always be him. "I know." The words came out little more than a whisper.

"So, call him," Savannah urged. "Call and talk things out."

She looked at her watch. "I planned to call him tonight, anyway. My guess is he's on a flight to Seattle right now, but even if he's not, this isn't a conversation I want to have on the road."

"Especially not tonight. Be careful driving home. You're headed into the mess, not away from it."

Sinclair signed off with a promise to be careful and strode through desultory rain to where she'd parked her car. The blanket of gray overhead hung low. A few beams of sunlight broke through in isolated patches to the south, like rays of hope. Her gaze sought them out in her rearview mirror as she drove onto the freeway, and she tried not to read anything into the fact that the skyline in front of her churned with clouds—thick and foreboding. Not a shred of light in sight.

Afternoon gave way to evening as she drove home, but the murky sky and constant rain made it an uninspiring transition from dusk to dark. She didn't normally mind the drive. Watching the sprawl of Atlanta thin out to suburbs, and then farms, and then miles of greenbelt dotted by the occasional signs for gas, food, Jesus, or Lake Winnepesaukah helped her shed the stress of the business side of her job. But tonight she just wanted to get home—for however much longer it would be home to her. The lawyer she'd retained to give her an opinion on her chances of fighting Ricky's termination of her land lease hadn't been too encouraging. Yes, the Pinkerton Family Trust might owe her damages for entering into a land lease they knew, or should have known, violated local zoning codes, but at the end of the day, the code was the code, and it would control. He was looking into the specific language to determine if she had any wiggle room given she used her building for business *and* residential purposes, but ultimately, she'd probably have to move.

A couple months ago, her world had been settled. Stable. Within her control. Now the status of her home was just one more uncertainty in a life suddenly rife with them. Maybe she was going to be a mother. She'd do whatever she could to make it happen. Of that much she was certain. Maybe she would have the man she loved at her side. She'd do whatever she could to make that happen, too, even if it meant uprooting herself from the place she considered home. Shane didn't. Yes, he'd let her believe their second chance included him coming back to stay, and he'd let her believe coming home was important to him, but considering how bleak the odds of her keeping her home looked at the moment, it could be the universe was trying to send her a message.

Maybe he didn't come back to Magnolia Grove, but he came back to you.

The epiphany flew from her mind when she reached the rise of the hill where the Whitehall Plantation stood, and through the steady curtain of rain her headlights picked up the outline of trucks and equipment sitting in the distance, beside long, parallel walls of mounded dirt.

"That bastard."

Ricky and team had wasted no time getting their golf course construction underway. Dammit, she still had over three weeks to move, according to his stupid notice. How much rain had they gotten? She slowed and took the turn to her drive. How much of it was being funneled down to her end of the creek? More importantly, how much water could her end of the creek hold before the banks overflowed?

Her high beams provided answers about three-quarters of the way to her house. A huge puddle covered the path, stretching from the tree-line on the left and continuing all the way to the other side of the drive. She slowed and steered the Tahoe through, listening as the muted sound of rubber cutting through water thinned to the tinny, hollow pings of waves splashing against her hubcaps. The water seemed to get deeper by the second. How much clearance did the Tahoe have? A foot? Eighteen inches? And how would *she* fare, knee-deep in water with a discernible downstream current?

Best not to find out. When the barn came into view, she gave the steering wheel a hard turn and drove up the slight slope on which the structure perched, lurching to a stop beside the big, double-hung sliding doors on the side. Her heart pounded as if she'd sprinted up the driveway. Sweat coated her cold skin. Three feet more, at most, and she'd have a wading pool for a first floor. She needed to…fuck…what *could* she do, except grab everything important, toss it in the back of the Tahoe, and drive to her parents'? Her mind raced through a list of things to gather—her sketchbooks, everything in the safe, her tools, her computer…oh God…so much. She launched herself out of the car and nearly lost her footing on the slick, muddy ground. Rain gear. A hysterical laugh tried to break free from somewhere beneath her pounding heart. Rain gear would be handy.

Stinging droplets pelted her skin and soaked her hair.

She pushed it out of her eyes and took a lunging step toward the barn. The blast of a horn brought her head around, and headlights momentarily blinded her.

A Campbell's Construction super-duty pickup lumbered up the slope. Another followed a few yards behind, and then a flatbed loaded with something. Mayor Campbell stepped out of the first truck, along with three beefy guys wearing work boots and rain ponchos. Campbell walked toward her while the other guys headed around to the bed of the truck.

"What the…" She swallowed, and tried again. "Mayor Campbell, what's going on?"

"I got a call from a friend of yours a couple hours ago, asking me to get a team out here with sandbags. These guys"—he pointed to the growing group of men assembling around the now-parked trucks—"are going to build you your own personal floodwall."

"Oh my God. That's amazing, but…" Questions poured in faster than she could process them. "I'm sorry. I don't know what's involved with this kind of thing. I'm not sure I can afford to have you do it, and even if I can, what's the point? It's a temporary solution. The next big rain will land me right back in this same predicament."

Campbell held up a hand. "Don't worry about the cost. Pinkerton is footing the bill, and there's a permanent solution in the works."

Okay. None of that made sense. "Ricky called and arranged for this?"

"Not exactly. He signed off on the check, but Pinkerton didn't put the wheels in motion." Campbell trailed off as a black Range Rover roared up the slope and skidded to a halt a few feet away.

An instant later, Shane stepped out. She blinked, struggling to wrap her head around the fact that he was… here. He closed in on them, his steps unfaltering, but his scruffy jaw, wrinkled jeans, and half-laced boots testified to a long day—or possibly days—leading him here. He shrugged out of a hip-length all-weather jacket as he walked. A black baseball cap bearing a Haggerty Consulting logo shielded his eyes from view, yet even so she knew they were locked on her.

Her knees went weak.

Mayor Campbell cleared his throat. "I'll let this guy explain." Then he clapped Shane on the shoulder and disappeared.

The Haggerty hat funneled the rain to the edge of the brim, where it rolled off in steady drops. He turned it backwards and then leaned toward her and wrapped his coat around her.

"What are you doing here?"

He met her stare. "I'm here to fix things, baby girl. Just like I promised."

• • •

Twenty-four hours, three flights, innumerable phone calls, and one dead-serious threat to beat the shit out of someone all paid off here and now with the stunned but *relieved* look on Sinclair's face. The stunned part wasn't too flattering. Obviously, she hadn't expected him to come through in her hour of need, but the relief told him everything he needed to know. Her world might be upending before her eyes, but his being here eased something inside her. She trusted him to try and make things right.

And he would. He was the man with the plan, and he had one for her—for them. He pulled his jacket more snugly around her.

"You arranged all this?" She gestured at the men springing into action around them.

"For starters."

"How?"

"Haggerty contacted me yesterday and told me Ricky had rammed the golf course permit through the planning commission and then fast-tracked the construction. I called in the big gun."

"The big gun? Mayor Campbell?"

"Bigger. I called Claudia Pinkerton and let her know her grandson was putting a piece of Magnolia Grove history in jeopardy with his new golf course. I figured the president of the Magnolia Grove Historical Society might object. Stridently. Let's just say she *prevailed upon* Ricky to get a crew down here ASAP and sandbag the place. Ricky's personal financial situation will suffer severe reverses if this structure takes any water damage."

He watched her lips twist into a fleeting smile at the idea of Claudia Pinkerton reading her grandson the riot act, but then she put a hand on his chest and looked up at him with serious eyes. "I appreciate the effort, and all the trouble you went to, Shane, but clearly you were right from the start. I'm now in a flood zone. If the resort's permit is valid, that's a permanent situation. I can't live behind a wall of sandbags forever. According to the city's zoning ordinances, I can't live here at all."

"I know." He covered her hand with his. "I have a plan for that, too."

"A three-phase plan?" Dark brows arched. "Isn't that where we started?"

Hopefully not where they ended. "You love this barn. I get that. You also own it. Every board. Every brick. So, we're going to move it—every board, every brick."

Her mouth fell open. "Move it where?"

"That's up to you, but…" This was where the plan got personal. He pulled her in closer and tipped her chin until their eyes met. "I just happen to hold the deed on the perfect spot. Big, quiet lot. Plenty of trees. It's zoned for residential use, and water encroachment isn't an issue."

She gripped his hand. "Are you serious? You'd let me put my barn on your lot?"

"Well, it's a little more complicated. There are some strings attached to my offer."

"I—" Her mouth worked for a moment, then she swallowed as if her throat had gone dry and started again. "Let's hear them."

"I come with the lot, Sinclair. Or rather, we do. I'm sorry I lied. I wasn't playing you so much as looking for a way to convince you to deal with me—and when you did, I fell for you all over again. Hard, and fast, like the first time, but this time there was no fucking chance I could walk away. I bought the lot thinking I wanted to hold onto an important piece of my past." He laughed. "I didn't realize until afterwards, when I was sitting there with a deed in my hand, I'd only owned up to half my motives. It wasn't just about the past. It was about the future. The whole truth is I wanted the lot because I want roots. I want a home. I want you. And I want this baby we've made. I don't have a hell of a lot of control over that part, but I'm in, Sinclair, for whatever ride life takes us on."

She blinked fast and wiped at her damp cheeks, which might be a bad sign, or just a by-product of the rain that fell in a steady shower around them. "You hate it here."

"No. As someone took the time to point out to me recently, I belong here. I haven't fought hard enough for my place, but that's going to change. I'm not leaving just because certain people would rather not have me around. I don't really give a shit if half the town thinks I'm trouble. I'm staying. So, what do you say, baby girl? You want to settle down with Magnolia Grove's least-favorite son?"

Her arms were around his neck and her body plastered to his before he finished asking the question. Triumph surged, only to recede just as quickly when her voice broke over something like a sob, and she said, "No."

He eased back and lowered his chin to get a look at her face. "Sinclair, I have to warn you, I'm going to do whatever it takes to change your—"

"No, you're *not* Magnolia Grove's least-favorite son. You've earned people's respect. All of this"—she gestured around them again—"proves my point. Claudia Pinkerton doesn't suffer fools, but she didn't doubt when you told her the barn was at risk. Mayor Campbell wouldn't rally a crew in the middle of a rainstorm to lay a bunch of sandbags just because Ricky showed up with his checkbook. He did it because of *you*. They trust you."

Maybe they did, and later, he might take a moment to appreciate the victory, but right now, he only cared about winning one person's respect. "What about you, Sinclair? Do *you* trust me?"

By way of answer, she came up on her toes and sealed her mouth to his. He cupped the back of her head and took everything—demanded everything—and didn't let her go until they were both panting. Once his breathing leveled off, he heard the whistles and catcalls over the soundtrack of falling rain and truck engines. He blocked them out and focused on the woman in his arms. "I know my timing could use a little work, but I'll take that as a yes."

She nodded. "Yes, I trust you. And yes, I want to settle down with the man I love." Her arms tightened around his waist, and she gave him a hard hug. "As for your timing, I'd say it's perfect."

Pride and relief washed through him, as tangible as the rain. "In that case, I've got one more question for you." He eased back and dug in his pocket. "Think you can turn this into a wedding ring?" He opened his hand to offer her the infinity symbol she'd made him for his eighteenth birthday.

She reached for it and then drew back when the platinum caught the light. "Oh my God." Shock sucked the strength from her voice, leaving only a whisper. "You still have it."

He shifted the artfully twisted wire so he held it between his thumb and forefinger. "The leather wore away a long time ago, but this"—he traced her lip with the precious metal—"this lasted. When you gave it to me, you promised me forever. I'm holding you to it."

This time there was no mistaking the tears in her eyes, but she smiled and took the symbol. A single, dark brow shot up. "What's your timeline?"

"Expedited," he answered and lowered his mouth to hers. "I've waited a decade already. I don't want to wait anymore. The rest of our forever starts now."

Epilogue

"Aw, baby, don't put your mouth on that," Shane heard his brother-in-law, Beau, warn. "You don't know where it's been."

He stepped through the tall glass doors that led from the back deck of the barn to the dining room in time to see his six-month-old daughter, April, bestow a wet mess of a kiss on Hunter Knox. The toddler in Hunter's other arm—his adopted daughter, Joy—giggled at the baby's sloppy affection and followed suit, depositing a smacking kiss on her father's cheek.

"That's right, girls. Ignore Uncle Beau." Hunter jiggled both kids and aimed a lazy grin at his friend. "He's just jealous 'cause you like me best." Then the blond man's nose wrinkled. He sniffed one girl, then the other. His grin turned conspiratorial and switched to Shane. "Hey, Uncle Beau, April's got a present for you."

Beau paused on his way to the fridge, snagged a diaper out of the bag on the table and winged it at Hunter like a Frisbee. "Man up, Uncle Hunter. You're her favorite."

Hunter turned to shield himself from the padded missile.

It bounced off his back and landed on the floor. "Huh? What's that, baby?" He held the infant higher in his arm, as if she whispered in his ear, and winked at Joy. "Nope, she definitely said, 'Uncle Beau, this one's for you.'"

Beau took a beer from the fridge and turned, but whatever reply he'd been about to offer got cut off by an enthusiastic, "Doooooown!" He had just enough time to place his beer on the table and catch his towheaded son, Ryder, before the turbo-powered ten-month-old jumped from the high chair. "Sorry, April, I'm busy keeping Savannah, Jr. out of a body cast."

"Nice catch," Shane joked as he passed Beau and headed toward Hunter. "I'll take her."

Hunter handed her over, but picked up the diaper on the floor and tossed it at Beau's head. "Multitask, motherfucker. We're supposed to be handling things, so this hard-up fool can set the scene out back and get himself laid for the first time in six months."

April cooed at Shane as he set her down on the changing mat lying on the floor in the living area. He smiled and touched his nose to her tiny one. "The scene is set, and we don't say the f-word in front of the kids, do we? No, we don't."

From behind him, Joy clapped her hands. "No fofo!"

"Shhh!" Hunter whispered and snuggled her.

Shane wasn't so easily silenced. "That's exactly right, Joy." With practiced skill, he changed the dirty diaper then bundled it up and lobbed it at Hunter.

Anticipating retaliation, the limber motherfucker ducked out of the way. "Missed me, bitch."

Shane shook his head and addressed his daughter. "We don't say the b-word, either. Also, for Uncle Hunter's information, it hasn't been six months since I've gotten laid." He turned back to April and lifted her into the air, so her little legs bicycled. "It's been six months since I've gotten laid without knowing one of us had to keep an ear out for you. Yes, we do, beautiful." He lowered her until their noses touched again. "We keep one ear tuned to you." She smiled and grabbed his hair, while he got to his feet. "But tonight, we're going to let Grandma and Grandpa do the honors. Aren't we?" He hoped so. If she refused to cooperate, he'd wasted his time putting an infant car seat in Grandma's car and setting a romantic scene in the backyard while Sinclair, Savannah, their mother, and Hunter's wife, Madison, took a day in Norcross to celebrate Savannah allowing Beau to impregnate her again.

"She'll be fine," Beau assured him as he held a small hand in each of his and slowly lowered his son to the floor. Ryder danced his bare feet over the sanded and polished planks. "Grandma and Grandpa survived a whole weekend with this one, and, unlike him, April's not actively trying to kill herself every two seconds. She'll be a walk in the park for them."

"Speaking of walks," Hunter nodded toward Ryder. "Little man's raring to go." Joy wriggled in her daddy's arms. "Okay, okay." He knelt and put her down. "Go on. Show him how it's done."

Joy scampered over to Ryder, eager to show off the walking skills she'd mastered during her vastly more experienced eighteen months of living. She stopped about a half foot away and held out her arms to the baby. "C'mere, Ry-Ry."

Ryder looked up at his dad. Beau shook his head. "Don't do it, cowboy. Your mother will skin me alive if she misses your first steps." But apparently, he was willing to risk a skinning, because he opened his hands so only Ryder's grip on his index fingers connected the two.

"I've got you covered." Hunter pulled his phone from his pocket and framed up the shot. "Aaand…we're rolling. Go on, Ry-Ry. Get her. Joy, honey, don't crowd him. Give him some room."

They all watched chubby hands slowly open. Beau straightened when Ryder let go of his fingers. The little guy balanced for a moment, looked around, and let out a hoot just to make sure he had everyone's attention. Shane mentally moved baby gates up on his home project list. Thankfully, Sinclair's spiral staircase had been repurposed and now connected the master bedroom to a roof deck, but the wide, wood-and-iron central stairway they'd installed when they'd redesigned the barn wasn't exactly baby safe.

Hunter started a drumroll. Ryder took a step toward Joy, staggered like a drunk for one ungainly second, and then toppled forward, taking his spotter down in the process.

"Uh-ohhh! Wipeout," Hunter called in an attempt to distract the kids from their tumble.

It didn't work. Ryder sucked in a breath and let loose an indignant holler. Joy immediately followed suit. Beau and Hunter hurried over.

Upset by the commotion, April joined in with an impressive wail. Shane bounced her in his arms. "Hey, now. What are *you* fussing for? You're just fine."

Over the din of three bawling infants, Shane heard the front door slide open. Perfect timing. The womenfolk were back, just when all hell broke loose. His well-crafted plans crumbled before his eyes. So much for a quick-and-painless handoff to Grandma before ushering everyone out and turning his attention to a slow and thorough seduction of his wife. "Whose boneheaded idea was it to set the kids up like dominoes?"

"Hunter's," Beau answered and pasted a smile on his face as the ladies walked in. Pretty, blond Madison appeared first, followed by Savannah, her mom, and Sinclair.

"Goodness." Madison quickened her pace. "What happened?" She was already shrugging her purse off her shoulder and preparing to take Joy.

"Everything's under control," Beau assured her.

Savannah came to her husband's side and inspected her red-faced son before giving Beau a skeptical look. "Uh-huh. Clearly, you guys have things under control."

"*We* do," Shane insisted, tipping his head toward Beau as Sinclair closed in on him. "This is Hunter's fault."

"Honey, don't believe them. I've got a video that proves different."

Madison cuddled her daughter, glanced through the glass doors to the backyard, and then shot a look at Shane. Her lips curved as she turned to Hunter. "Show me later, 'kay? We've got to get going, or we'll be late for the…thing."

He'd always liked Madison. Even more so when everyone sprang into motion at her comment and started gathering up kids and gear.

"What thing?" Sinclair asked.

"Oh, you know…" Savannah gestured vaguely and grabbed Ryder's diaper bag. "The thing. We've got a thing. Thanks for driving today."

Sinclair's mother looked at him, one brow arched in silent question. He gave her a small nod.

She cleared her throat. "Sinclair, honey, do you have that necklace we talked about? The one I might want to borrow?"

"Um, sure." She glanced uncertainly at the flurry of activity around her. "Let me run upstairs and get it. Don't everyone run off. I'll be right back."

He watched as Sinclair climbed the stairs and sailed along the open hallway. As soon as she disappeared into the bedroom, everyone rushed to the door. A speed round of hugs and kisses transpired, and then Cheryl lifted April from his arms. "We're gone." She kissed his cheek and stepped onto the porch. "Have a good night."

"You, too. Call if she gets cranky. I'll come get her."

His mother-in-law laughed. "This sweet little girl doesn't have a cranky bone in her body."

"Sometimes she—"

"Hush. She'll be fine."

"All right. Let us take you and Bill to dinner next week as a thank-you."

"No need." Cheryl kissed the top of April's head. "You want to thank us, just give us another one of these."

• • •

Sinclair peered downstairs to find Shane standing alone in the middle of the living room. "Where is everyone?"

He met her at the foot of the stairs, and she couldn't help noticing the little gleam in his eye. "Gone."

"Seriously? Even Mom?"

He nodded and absently stretched, raising his arms over his head and causing his T-shirt to ride up so she caught a glimpse of rippling abs. "Even your mom."

"Well, jeez." She let her eyes stray to the front of his jeans for a second—just long enough to put a depraved flutter in her stomach. It was very quiet. Was April napping? Maybe they could squeeze in some grown-up time if they hurried. She set the freshwater pearl and rock crystal necklace she'd fetched from her jewelry box down on an end table. "Guess she didn't want to borrow this after all."

"She decided to borrow something else instead." He took her hand and led her through the living area to the dining room, stopping to pick up one of April's pacifiers from under the table. Sinclair opened her mouth to ask what her mom had borrowed, but got distracted by the way the move showcased his ass. His jeans rode low, revealing twin dimples bracketing the base of his spine and a generous band of pale skin below his tan line. Was he wearing underwear? She envisioned licking the enticing area from dimple to dimple and then tugging his jeans down and sinking her teeth into unprotected flesh.

When he straightened, she forced her tongue down from the roof of her mouth. "Something of Savannah's?"

He tossed the pacifier onto the table. "Nope."

Before she could follow up on that cryptic reply, he went on. "Did you enjoy the spa?"

"I did." Then, because he was looking at her like he knew she'd been thinking about biting his ass, she turned to face him and slowly smiled. "What's not to enjoy about having a brawny blond named Eric massage all my kinks out?"

A scowl carved a notch between his brows. "I can think of several things, actually." He stepped close, trapping her between the table and his body. "Exactly where were these kinks?"

"Hmm, you know. Here and there...ohhh..." Her breath whooshed out when he reached under her skirt, and big, capable hands squeezed her ass.

His lips menaced her ear. "Here? You feel a little tight right here."

"Um. Gosh, he might not have gotten out *all* my kinks."

"Good help is so hard to find." His grip relaxed, then tightened again, bringing her up on her toes. "I guess I'll have to finish the job."

"I guess you will. Where's April?"

"Your mom borrowed her." As he spoke, he kneaded her flesh, setting off hot waves of sensation that rolled through her, making it impossible for her to focus on his words.

"I don't understand." Her vision blurred as his fingers followed the line of her thong. "B-borrowed her?"

He nodded, and his unshaven jaw tickled skin. "Just for tonight."

"Oh." Uncertainty flared at the prospect of the baby

spending the night without them but subsided as Shane read her mind and murmured, "She'll be fine."

She would. Of course, she would, and it was sweet of him to plan an evening for them together. Then a muscular thigh slid between hers, and all thoughts of sweetness flew out of her head. He lifted her closer, so her breasts crashed into his chest. A long, thick ridge settled heavily against her stomach. She couldn't hold back a moan.

"So, about those kinks…"

She reached between their bodies and slipped her hand into his jeans. Hallelujah, no underwear. He shuddered as she closed her fist around him. "I'm afraid they're quite extensive."

"No problem." He took her hands and linked them around his neck then hauled her into his arms. Her skirt rode up as she wrapped her legs around his waist. "I planned for that."

She leaned in and bestowed little bites along his jaw. "Did you?"

"You know me. Close your eyes."

She did, and the world whirled. He carried her out the back door and down the deck steps. Evening closed in around them—warm air, alive with the chirp of crickets and the flash of fireflies. When he stopped and slowly lowered her to her feet, she didn't need to open her eyes to know where she was. Their tree.

He moved away from her. Something rustled. "Turn around and open your eyes."

She did, and her heart swelled at the sight of him standing there, bathed in the soft glow of lantern light, holding back a curtain of willow limbs to reveal a picnic basket and a blanket.

"There's no place like home."

"Wow. You really did have a plan for tonight."

"I've been planning to get you back under this tree for a while." He arched a brow at her. "*You're* the one who came home feeling kinky."

A memory of what he'd promised her last time he'd talked about getting her on a blanket under their tree filtered through her mind. Her knees wobbled and her cheeks heated. "How kinky are you planning to get?"

He laughed and took her hand. "I'm open to suggestions, but"—his expression sobered as he led her under the canopy—"if you're game, I thought we might try to give April a little brother or sister."

Her heart stuttered in her chest and then took off at double time. "Do you want to?"

He nodded. "It's not risk free, and we could go the scientific route if you'd rather, but the old-fashioned way worked out pretty well last time around."

"Yes, it worked out perfectly," she managed around the lump in her throat and walked over to him. "I'd love to."

He wrapped his arms around her and lowered his head. "I love you, baby girl. You're mine. My past, present, and future. You're my everything."

"Good to know, since I feel the same way."

His slow grin heated her belly. "That was my plan."

Acknowledgments

I'd like to start by thanking you, dear reader. Arguably, my friends and family *have* to chime in every once in a while and say "attagirl," if for no other reason than their own peace of mind. The talented people at Entangled are kinda duty bound to help create the best books possible. (They go above and beyond the call of duty, but more on that later). Readers, however, don't have to choose my books. You're not obligated to tell me or anyone else if you enjoy them. I am thrilled and humbled when readers do. I'm extra thrilled to have gotten to know some of you through social media and book signings. You ladies inspire me (occasionally with pictures of hot, half-naked men, and words cannot express how very deeply I appreciate it), you make me laugh, and sometimes you even make me cry—but in a good way! So thank you, readers. Feel free to request this appreciation in the form of a free drink the next time you see me.

Additional thanks and free drinks to:

My editor, Heather Howland, for always seeing past what's on the page, to what should be on the page, and gently prodding me to get it there.

Liz, Melanie, Curtis, Kaitlyn and the rest of the Entangled team, for being the sh*t.

Robin and Hayson, for being the best writing buddies (aka drinking buddies) a girl could have.

My family and friends, for all the attagirls. xoxo

About the Author

Wine lover, sleep fanatic, and *USA Today* Bestselling Author of sexy contemporary romance novels, Samanthe Beck lives in Malibu, California, with her long-suffering but extremely adorable husband and their turbo-son. Throw in a furry ninja named Kitty and Bebe the trash talking Chihuahua and you get the whole, chaotic picture.

When not dreaming up fun, fan-your-cheeks sexy ways to get her characters to happily-ever-after, she searches for the perfect cabernet to pair with Ambien.

If you love sexy romance, one-click these steamy
Brazen releases...

ALL I WANT IS YOU
a novel by Candace Havens

Hawke will do anything to protect the family business, even marry a ballerina with too many secrets. Thankfully, they only have to play pretend for two months, because the more time they spend together, the more Hawke starts reconsidering letting Amy go.

MAKE ME BEG
a Men of Gold Mountain novel by Rebecca Brooks

Mackenzie Ellinsworth has a plan for how opening her own bar and restaurant should go. Not in that plan: a ripped and rugged playboy stepping in to take over. The two of them can't agree on anything—except how scorching hot their chemistry is.

A Moment of Madness
a Boston Alibi novel by Brooklyn Skye

Sailor Carlson is back in Boston to check out the Alibi, her late father's bar. What she finds is Ryan Edwards, the Alibi's current owner, a bearded, grumpy hottie. Ryan likes Sailor enough for nameless sex on the kitchen counter—until he realizes who she is.

Falling for the Bad Girl
a Cutting Loose novel by Nina Croft

Detective Nathan Carter is a cop, through and through. But his work ethic—and libido—are thrown off balance when he heads up the case against jewel thief, Regan Malloy. Because with one sizzling look, she's had him hot and hard ever since. But now Regan's out of prison and hoping to start over. It's inevitable that they'll meet up again—in bars, hotels…and hotel beds. Still, it's just desire. If they give it enough time, it'll burn itself out. Because a good boy and a bad girl can't possibly make it work. Or can they?

ENTANGLED
BRAZEN

Made in United States
North Haven, CT
21 October 2022

25751695R00146